Stealing Home

SHARON HASHIMOTO

Stealing Home

GRID BOOKS | BOSTON

Grid Books
Boston, MA
grid-books.org

COVER IMAGE:
Kenjiro Nomura (1896–1956)
Untitled, circa 1952
Oil on board, 19 × 24 in.
Private collection
Courtesy of the estate of Kenjiro Nomura
and Cascadia Art Museum, Edmonds, WA

ISBN: 978-1-946830-22-7

ACKNOWLEDGMENTS
Some stories were previously published: "Stealing Home" in
American Fiction, "English as a Second Language" in *Crab Orchard
Review*, "Slippage" in *Indiana Review*, "A Good Face" in *Louisiana
Literature*, "Kibo's Cats" in *Moss*, "Blue Jay Feather," and West
Coast Blues" in *North American Review*, "No Further Than You
Can Throw" in *The Rambler*, "Sworn" in *River Styx*, "Vindaloo"
in *Shenandoah*, and "The Wind Against Him" in *The Tampa Review*.

For Michael,

the other half of the story

Contents

English as a Second Language

Goro knew more English than he let on. After forty years in the United States, he had learned it was easier to nod his head and point at what he wanted: pipe tobacco, Kleenex, his walking stick. He could always pretend he didn't understand during the times when his daughter, Margaret, brought those fancy croissants as a treat. He didn't like all the air pockets he'd bite into. What he wanted was the heavy old-fashioned doughnuts he used to eat with black coffee. For show, he would tear her flaky pastries into tiny bits as if he were actually eating them.

Lately, his whole family, even his wife, had started to treat him like a puppet—bundling him up in his robe, picking his hand up and closing his fingers around a teacup. "Achh," he snapped at her and pulled his hand away. He knew what things were on the table—plate, cup, utensils—even if he couldn't see so well. He heard his wife's quick intake of breath sucked between her teeth as she held back an angry retort. Sometimes, he thought, it was a good thing that his hearing was so keen.

"Is Grandpa mad? Why did he do that?"

"I think I made the tea too hot." He hated the way they whispered around him. Then more loudly, as if speaking to a stranger, his wife said, "Goro, I'm sorry. Let me get some ice to cool it down."

Defiantly he held his head up, sat erect, and stared past the voices, focusing on the kitchen clock steadily ticking above their heads. There was no reason for the way she talked at him—

saying things like "wipe your mouth" —as if she were giving orders to a half-wit child.

Jeffrey, his daughter's son, was sitting across the table from him. He could still see the blurred motion of the chopsticks shoveling rice into a mouth. He could smell the spinach in sesame seed oil and the hot batter of tempura. She had gone all out to please the boy, making food that didn't seem too strange. Did this boy even know about putting mochi and small oranges out for the dead?

There was the small clink of an ice cube hitting the rim of the cup. He waited while she put food on his plate. When she was done, she put her hand on his shoulder and said in Japanese, two days the little one will be staying with us. He picked up a drumstick with his fingers and started to bite into the flesh. He smacked his lips as he chewed. For a while, the three of them ate without speaking.

"Jeffrey, why don't you tell Grandpa what we saw at the grocery store today."

Goro could hear the kitchen chair creak as the boy shifted his weight. Slowly he started, drawing out his sentences: "Well, there was that smelly fish with the big head. We bought cucumbers and eggs and tiny tomatoes..."

The boy spoke with no enthusiasm. His words seemed flat to Goro, like the black and white letters pressed into a book. He remembered how mad he was when the white storekeeper told him he was slurring his "D"s and "T"s at the end of his words. The chicken was cold in the middle so Goro left it on his plate. Picking up his coffee mug with both hands, Goro slurped noisily—only partly listening to his grandson's voice.

Napping and feeling warm in a small patch of winter sunshine, he blinked open his eyes and just for a second thought he saw the two of them. Hair up in a tight bun, she was wearing a faded dress. Her hands were busy with a crochet needle and bright yellow yarn. The boy, wrists pushing at his bowl cut hair, was sitting on the floor, fingers clenched around a crayon, butcher paper spread in front of him. He heard the tapping of the crayon as Jeffrey put polka-dots on his picture. Then everything blurred again as a cloud blew past the sun.

On a good day, he used to be able to read the Japanese edition of *Reader's Digest* with his magnifying glass. All those black characters against the white light of the page. He had wanted to fill up his eyes the same way he used to stare into the center of the sun. The same sun that once striped his exposed back and shoulders as he swung bales of hay onto a green pickup truck. Then, when he looked up, shading his eyes, all he could see was flat brown land stretching all the way to the foothills of the Cascades.

Once, when his wife and daughter thought he was sleeping, they were careless and their voices grew loud. They spoke all the time now in English.

"If only it hadn't been his eyesight, if he had gone deaf instead," Margaret was saying. "Ma, I don't know how you manage."

He could almost hear his wife's head bow in agreement. "He has his good moments and his bad. But he doesn't walk much anymore; says he doesn't want the cane. Last time, he lost his way in the back yard. Got stuck between the garbage cans. I found him on his hands and knees in the coffee grounds. He doesn't want my help." He heard her add: "Sometimes I wonder about his mind." His lost vision had made her bold.

She was bending now, over the picture their grandson had drawn. "That's a good bird, Jeffrey. But why do you use so much black?"

"Grandma! It's night-time. And that's a pterodactyl—you know, a flying dinosaur."

It was easy for Goro to close his eyes, take deeper breaths, and pretend his darkness was the same as a dream.

He knew his grandson didn't want to touch him when she asked Jeffrey to bring him his pipe and tobacco.

"Do I have to?" Jeffrey asked, his voice almost a whisper.

Standing up, he went to get his pouch himself. As his fingers skimmed the wall, he thought maybe the boy was afraid of his papery soft skin, the hairy mole that grew out of his chin. Maybe he had that old man smell of phlegm and uselessness that his own grandfather had had. His grandson was only six. Margaret, his middle daughter, had waited a long time to have this one. Jeffrey wouldn't know that he used to plow half a field, then come home after sunset to sharpen tools for the next day. It was hard work to make enough money for a wife and five kids. But he was good at making do with what he had.

He hadn't really noticed when his vision had started to tunnel in. Now, during the day, he walked in a kind of constant twilight—what one might find inside a cave. Before, in his middle years, he had had flashes in his eyes that he foolishly mistook for extra energy. He knew the doctor's medicine wouldn't do any good; it was too late for the drops that stung his eyes. His boys and close friends had talked him into selling off a few acres of the farm at a time as his sight slowly failed. His world had shrunk down to four rooms in the house.

It was five small steps towards the hallway. There was a smell of something weed-like tickling his nose. His fingers, feeling the surface of the dining room bureau, bumped into a vase and sent it spinning. "Baka!" he shouted, jerking his fingers back at the same time he heard the glass shatter on the floor. For a second, he imagined sharp reds, oranges, yellows—all somehow electric. It was his own stupid mistake; he should never have sent his hands out wandering beyond his sight. He started to kneel but his wife's arms were under his elbow, guiding him back to a chair.

"Be careful of the glass," he heard her tell their grandson. Then, in a whisper, "Grandpa didn't know. He doesn't see very well..."

He could feel his grandson pull back, deeper into the shadows. Maybe the child was afraid he'd set himself on fire.

Sometimes she snored as she lay on her back beside him—little snuffs and snorts punctuated the night. Sometimes he'd finger a fold of her cotton nightgown. Far away, a dog gave five sharp barks then stopped. He would have to wait some hours for the high-pitched beep of the alarm clock to start her day. He could feel the room's coldness on his face.

Tomorrow, maybe Mas would come by with a steelhead he had caught in the Nasalle River. They could sit and drink a beer while they talked about the weather and what crops were planned for the spring sowing. Then he remembered that Mas had moved to Hawai'i three years ago to be with his kids. His wife had read a letter that said Mas was now in a retirement home. Mas, who had been a good ten years younger than he.

In the living room, something was whimpering. Then he remembered the boy, bunked down on the sofa. He rolled onto his side towards the edge of the bed, but his wife continued to snore. It had been a long day. His daughter's son was easily bored, wanting to watch cartoons all the time on a color television set. Things were different in a small town, she had tried to explain to him. There was never a good enough answer to his plaintive "why?" At six, his own sons had helped box tomatoes from the field. Jeffrey could have been feeding the chickens or gathering eggs, making himself useful. His own sons had been afraid of folk tales told late at night of the Taira massacre back in old Japan, of spirits returned from the dead.

Quietly, he got up to make his way towards the living room. With one hand stretched out in front of him, he took small steps so as not to trip on the carpet. During the day, he could at least make out the shape of things. Night turned everything into one black wall. He thought to himself, what must the boy feel—waking up in a strange house, and not even in a bedroom. Was his grandson afraid of the dark? Goro remembered his own childhood fear of a ghost-like willow tree, the limbs searching the room for him.

"Jeff-ie?" he whispered loudly. He coughed and hacked up mucus to clear his voice. Maybe the boy didn't understand his broken English. "Jeff-ie? You al-righ?" he called again. The crying died down. Goro stopped and tilted his head to listen.

He counted out fifteen steps and banged his shin on a low stool. The furniture made a loud scraping noise as it skidded across the hardwood floor. There was a small scared intake of breath. Waving his hands in front of him, he called again. But now he had lost his bearings and his voice took on a sharp note of panic: "Jeff-ie!" he yelled.

All the boy had to do was answer, but he was remaining perfectly still, hiding like a scared fawn in the darkness. He imagined Jeffrey would have his legs pulled up beneath him, his arms trying to fold himself into a tight ball. Goro's hands followed the nubby back of the sofa until they connected with something warm. Jeffrey gave a short shrill scream.

"Stay a-way from me!!" his grandson roared. Goro knew he was an old man as he tried to wrap his arms around the flailing boy but he was pushed away. "No, no!! I want my mom! I want my mom-my!"

And then the lights were switched on. It was like something

had exploded in his eyes. He couldn't tell if the room around him was in black or white. He blinked, trying to separate the sounds of a boy's bare feet running from his own ragged breathing. Then his wife spoke, half in English, half in Japanese. "Yakamashi! Why all this noise? What's going on?" The words were sharp, demanding.

He could sense Jeffrey hiccupping, breath catching in his throat. He pictured the child's arms enclosed around his wife's thick legs, the fabric of her robe and gown protecting him. Jeffrey's muffled words were spoken against her knees: "He was going to grab me." He imagined his grandson's index finger pointed towards his heart.

Sitting like a child on the cold floor, he crossed his legs beneath him. Goro remembered the long necks of evil phantoms and their pale wispy hair. He could hear their keening in his ears. He knew they slept during the day in the trunks of gnarled trees, emerging at dark to eat the kidneys of dead people. "Baku desu," he murmured to himself. He realized he was nothing but some horrid ghost who haunted an old woman during the day. At night, he came to suck a boy's sleep dry of his dreams. He couldn't stop the half-sob rising up his throat. Bowing his head into his hands, he was glad he couldn't see.

No Further Than You Can Throw

Rotating the cereal bowl, Cedric swiped out the center with his striped dish towel and stacked it with the others on the kitchen counter. He picked up the frying pan next and let the water, pooled in the curves, run-off into a tumbler. He'd managed to collect almost half a glass this time while his mother had been in her bedroom, dressing for work. "Kids, I'm leaving now," he heard her announce. Then there was the sound of hangers in the hallway closet, of keys jingling. She'd be waving at Janet as his little sister shut the front door behind her. "Bye, Mom," Cedric breathed out, wondering if she even heard him at all in her rush to catch the bus. Shaking off the utensils, he dropped each spoon and fork in the drawer with a clatter. At least now he could get on with his other chores. He hated wiping dishes.

Cedric hung the wet towel on the oven handle, then paused to peer into his sack lunch, wrinkling his nose at the smell of seaweed and rice. Two cellophane-wrapped triangles lay side-by-side. Shrimp and shoyu filling was his favorite, but Cedric knew his mother had been hurried last night. He had watched her seed and pack a pickled plum to place inside the rice—the deep maroon juices bleeding into the white kernels. Besides the triangles, there was a teriyaki thigh and drumstick, salted cucumber sticks and a banana.

Rebecca and Elizabeth and all those other white kids were sure to stare and mutter "Yuck, what's *that* you're eating?" From the living room, Cedric could hear a stuttering Elmer Fudd as he closed the window over the kitchen sink. He despised Bugs Bunny and those buck teeth. His younger sister, Janet, was probably on her stomach in her corduroy jumper, lying in front of the television set as she watched the early morning J. P. Patches Show. Usually, she'd have one knee-high stocking in her hand, the other on her foot. If his Dad had been there, he'd yell at her to sit in a chair like a proper lady. Instead, Cedric just shook his head.

Maybe if he peeled the banana skin real slow between tiny sips of his milk, he could make his stomach believe it was full during the lunch hour. Later, he could hide underneath the playground bleachers and enjoy the meal. It was bad enough that his father barbered Cedric's hair, shaving everything down to a fine one-inch fuzz that made his ears look even bigger than they were.

But that was why Mom had taken the job in the steno pool for the Veterans' Administration Hospital—to save money and maybe buy a second car. Whenever he phoned her at work, her usually quiet voice would rise to a whine: *Is this really important? You're thirteen years old, big enough to be in charge until I get home.* It was Cedric's job to check the stove and doors, to make certain everything was safe before he escorted Janet to her girlfriend's house across the street and he went on to Dunlop Junior High. Cedric shoved his fingers into his rear pocket to feel for the two folded dollar bills he needed for bread, butter, and a carton of eggs.

Dad did okay as one of the many wiring workers on the Boeing 727 jets. On some Sundays afternoons, Dad would pile them all into the car and they would go for a drive around Seward Park where Cedric knew all the rich Jewish kids from his school lived, the sons and daughters of lawyers and doctors. Dad would pass "Janet's Tree"—the madrona that each year tilted closer to the water, each wind storm breaking off new limbs. The old 1957 Ford would drive up the woodsy hairpin turns until they emerged at the top of the ridge with its pricey view homes, some with tennis courts and manicured hedges. "Lots of lawn to mow on that one," Dad would tease Cedric, his brown and callused finger pointing to a huge picture window of a two-story home. Mom and Janet would *ooh* and *ahh* at the bay windows and huge open porch, dreamily murmuring about swimming pools in the back yard.

Though he had smiled, Cedric had thought: *At least I wouldn't have to live in the basement.* Every morning on his way up to the kitchen, he had to pass rows of wet laundry his mother and sister had hung up the night before. He pulled tight and locked the sticky door to the "cold room" they used as a pantry off the side of the kitchen where they kept the garbage can full of Calrose Rice and six-packs of Shasta pop. He couldn't help but notice how this addition was falling away from the main foundation. He was going to attend the University of Washington—just like Dad wanted him to. But Cedric knew that when he grew up, he was going to be an engineer—a guy who'd *design* the jets his father worked on. And one day, he was going to drive a fancy new Lincoln Continental and live in a house in Seward Park.

If he were to make enough money, no one would be able to tell him what to do. Not the snobby girls from his math class, who wore blue on Jewish holidays; the ones who got time off from school. The ones who made fun of Cedric's haircut and who held their noses when he ate his lunch.

After Cedric put out the milk bottles and carefully locked the side door behind him, he laid the back of a hand on each stove burner to double check that they were off. The long arrow of the kitchen clock was ticking towards 8:00. The way his father talked, the Boeing machinists would have been crawling in and out of the 727 airplane bodies, wiring lights for the past hour. "These new guys," Dad had complained last night, "bunch of Fili-pinos. We have to fix their sloppy work." Grabbing their lunches, Cedric went to the hallway closet, then to the living room where he threw his sister's navy wool coat at her. He watched as one sleeve swatted her face, but her eyes never left the television screen. Elmer Fudd was aiming his shotgun toward the bridge of Bugs Bunny's nose. "Got your library books?" he asked. "What about your homework?"

Janet barely turned her head to glance up at him. "I want to watch this." By now, Bugs Bunny had stuck the pointy end of a carrot into the barrel of Elmer Fudd's gun.

Cedric walked over to his sister's side and nudged her with the toe of his tennis shoe. "Janet," he said. "I'm not kidding. Get your stuff together *now*." He prodded her with a little more force.

"Okay, okay," she mumbled. Slowly she stood, grabbing the coat by the collar and half-dragging it as she walked backwards, one hand feeling for the hallway, still watching the cartoon as she made her way to the bedroom.

On the television screen the shotgun exploded, and a wide-eyed Elmer Fudd stood with his face smeared with soot, the barrel splintered into shapes like the petals of a daisy. Cedric hit the off button and watched the picture screen flip twice, then narrow into a tiny point of light that gradually disappeared. Where had he put the keys?

A light rapping began at the front door—almost as if someone wasn't sure of the address. But then the doorbell rang, the sudden two-note *ding-dong* booming through the living room. Cedric jumped a little, then took three quick strides. His hand was already sliding back the safety chain when something stopped him. His first thought had been that either Mom or Dad had come back home. But why would they ring the doorbell? The bell seemed louder the second time as Cedric put his eye to the peephole.

Framed by the rounded curve of glass, a young black face stared down at the welcome mat, his eyebrows slightly raised. *Just a grammar school kid*, Cedric thought. *I can handle him.* The boy's hair was cut neat and short. He carried books under one long arm. Cedric watched as the boy shifted his weight from foot to foot, glancing back over his shoulder.

Cedric opened the door part way, standing behind it as he used his body to block the view into the house. There was the sucking, sticking noise the wood always made—and then the cold morning air brushed Cedric's face.

The boy looked startled, his eyes taking in Cedric's short-sleeved shirt and khakis. "Excuse me," he began, half-swallowing the words. "Does Janet Fujino live here?"

From where the driveway ended, at the edge of the fence, Cedric could see two other young boys watching. They were black, too. One of them grinned, playfully hitting his friend in the shoulder. Their laughter seemed raucous, sucking up all the quiet of his neighborhood. Cedric glanced from the two boys to the one standing on his front porch. "What if she does?" he answered. He didn't like the way those eyes refused to look away. Even though he stood a foot taller than any of them, Cedric didn't like the idea that they were a group.

"Janet and I have Mrs. Rosenblatt for third grade," the boy continued. To Cedric's ear, the "Mrs." came out sounding like slang. Cedric waited, giving no sign of response—only shifting one hand to rest on his hip. He thought of his father firmly turning away "those kinds of people" who sold raffle tickets door-to-door—the sort of deal where you just knew you'd be wasting your hard-earned money. The boy's lips parted in surprise. Maybe he was wondering if this was the right house. But then he brightened at the sound of Janet's voice, yelling that she couldn't find her shoe. "That's her. That's Janet! Tell her that I'm Alfred—Alfred from school," he insisted, trying to peer around Cedric and the door.

Janet usually brought home good citizenship marks on her report cards. His sister was probably friends with this Alfred the way he was friends with the Filipino and black guys in gym. He would cheer for any guy on his team who spiked a winning point in volleyball. Sometimes, Cedric would mumble a brief "hi" to them in the halls between classes. With a sideways nod in Janet's direction, he asked: "What do you want with my sister?"

The boys loitering beside the fence post had stopped laughing and were watching intently. Alfred took a deep breath. "I'd like to walk her to school."

Cedric's fingers massaged the space between his eyebrows. The skin felt rippled. In Alfred's eight-year-old voice, he heard a kind of admiration that sent a tremor down his spine. Cedric knew his father would be outraged. How many times had he heard Dad say: "Look at all those cars and refrigerators piled up in their yards." Or "See how one of them will stop their car in the middle of the street. They always make you wait until they finish talking to their friends." His father's angry tone echoed in Cedric's head, even though he knew people like Charles Hughes and Leonard Thomas who weren't like that at all.

"Please," Alfred said, the long curve of eyelashes blinking once. His face was smooth, the lips lightly parted. Cedric noticed that Alfred's skin tone wasn't really black, but a dark shade of brown that seemed to lighten at the curves of his cheekbones and chin. This boy didn't seem anything like Leonard, who'd sit up straight in the first row of the class, raising his hand whenever their history teacher asked a question.

Alfred started to lean forward like he was about to take a step into the house. That's when Cedric realized what was different; the boy didn't have the right attitude. *He's probably the kind who copies someone else's homework*. Cedric was certain that he didn't want his little sister to be walking with Alfred to school.

At first, Cedric shook his head lightly, barely whispering. Alfred leaned in closer, as if not quite believing what he'd heard.

Slowly, his voice growing loud, huskier, Cedric repeated: "You got the wrong address."

Alfred's right palm rose up. "I just heard Janet's voice!"

"No," Cedric said, backing away and closing the door. He stood staring at the rectangular shape and wood finish for a long moment. His eyes had been focused on Alfred's hand; the slender bones that made it seem bigger than a child's. Then Cedric glanced towards Janet's room where he could still hear her scuffling on the floor, maybe looking for a saddle shoe under the bed. She was such a baby, always happy with her Chatty Cathy dolls—paying no mind to the neighborhood their family lived in. He told himself: *Mom, Dad—they would have done the same thing.* Cedric counted to ten, hoping the boy had enough sense to get off the porch, rejoin his friends. He heard his nose whistle as he took a deep breath and a final look out the peephole.

Past the blur of Alfred's head, Cedric imagined stretched fingers. He wondered if the boy had left a mark on his front door. He thought about his baseball bat downstairs in his room.

Cedric jumped as Janet's voice suddenly called out. "Found it! Ced, it's on my foot now. I'm tying the laces." He could hear the echo of Elmer Fudd's voice as his sister added: "Cwa-zy shoe!"

He gave himself a little shake, then brushed past the sofa to stand beside the venetian blinds. Through the horizontal slats, he could make out Alfred and his friends—standing apart, like different players on opposing basketball teams before the tip-off. One boy pointed his index finger to the house and said something loud. Cedric winced. He could hear the noise even through the glass pane. He'd seen black kids shooting hoops on the school grounds, shoving and laughing and yelling. Their voices would grow harsh with accusations and swear words so rough Cedric couldn't tell if they were playing or fighting.

Alfred was looking down at the sidewalk, his tennis shoe nudging something in the curb grass. Cedric frowned. That kid might have been telling his friends what happened. Cedric felt his neck grow hot. How could Alfred not know this would happen? One friend shook his head and elbowed his way around Alfred, up the hill and towards the school. The other boy lingered with Alfred for a minute or two, finally running past the willow tree to catch up. Cedric felt his lips move: *Two down, one to go.*

His head turned in the direction his friends had disappeared, Alfred kept looking up. Cedric couldn't understand why Alfred was being so stubborn, why he wouldn't leave. Maybe the boy's friends were calling to him to hurry. Maybe they were going to shoot some baskets on the school's playground before classes started at 9:00. But Janet's classmate just stood there; his eyes seemed to focus on the lumps in the gravel driveway.

Instead, Alfred bent over, picking up the object he'd been toeing. The boy tossed the marble-sized stone up, and caught it. Cedric imagined the boy's fingers beginning to squeeze the rough shape. Alfred looked at the house, eyes narrowed like he wasn't sure what he was going to do. Finally, Alfred's shoulders slumped, the stone seeming to grow heavy and dragging the hand down.

Cedric pulled quickly away from the window. He closed his eyes and pictured Alfred's face, thick lips pressed tight in anger, forehead furrowed like he was about to explode. The rock, big as a half-dollar, sails towards the house. The picture window cracks.

Cedric rubbed his hands against his pant legs. He imagined his father stabbing a finger at the jagged ends of glass, yelling. He saw himself hanging his head, mumbling that it wasn't his fault. After all, what could he do when there'd been a whole gang of them, three boys bigger than he, and Janet to protect? She'd been afraid, hiding in her bedroom. And he had done everything that he could, politely explaining that his little sister was ill. They just didn't like what they heard. Who could tell why those kinds of people, those kurombo, did what they did.

A Good Face

Heart Mountain, 1944

I.

Hanako made her son, Henry, sit next to her at the long table in the mess hall. She watched as he hung his head, staring at his lap and obeying her commands: here, sit, eat. Cold and lumpy mush and toast were their breakfast.

She felt the stares against the back of her neck. Each mouthful was like the lump of retorts she held on her tongue before swallowing them down. No one could see her thoughts and she wasn't going to make them public. Angry words were no defense. She needed to show Henry and his accusers, to put on a good face. In spite of any table of onlookers, Hanako held her back erect, her head up, both feet on the ground. She scolded Henry for not putting a napkin on his lap and coached him to take smaller bites. Usually children Henry's age, those second graders, hung out together, but she'd seen one woman stop, point with her chin and murmur "not there" while shooing her boy away from their table.

Hanako knew her son was bored and lonely since school let out. But Henry needed to earn back his good name. He'd always been an inquiring boy, wanting to know what part of the chicken was the wish bone and who was taking care of their Ten Cent store back home, full of household goods and food stuffs. More recently, he'd begun to whine "how long do we have to stay here" as they stood on their side of the barbed wire fence. As his mother, she was responsible. She hushed him, telling him she'd explain later. Everything, Henry complained, was later. The problem, Hanako knew, was that nowhere was private.

When Hanako stood up to carry her tray to the dishwashers, she saw Mrs. Adachi and Mrs. Fujino glance up at her, their hands not even shielding their mouths, to whisper together. When they saw Henry passing by, they turned away.

Hanako told herself she didn't care what the people in her block said. Most were strangers from California. Peach and strawberry farmers. The kind who would eventually find something else to gossip about. Some tidbit like the father who went to the Methodist gatherings, the one who was so worried about money. He'd asked his daughter to marry his bachelor friend who was financially better off. Arranged marriages were something the Issei understood.

But these teenagers! She couldn't believe how some girls painted their lips bright red and threw themselves at boys. In the middle of the cafeteria, some young people were loudly complaining again about wanting to eat good food like pancakes or waffles. They wanted sweets like strawberry jam from their families' farms. How they dreamed of hamburgers and ice cream sundaes. The best breakfast stuff, they argued, the maple syrup and bacon was kept for the block managers who everybody knew hoarded goods or sold them on the black market.

Hanako shook her head. For fifteen- and sixteen-year-olds, they knew nothing. She'd seen them reading those gossip magazines like *Glamour* in the canteen. Most girls were experimenting with pin curls and learning how to jitterbug. One of them giggled, while the others shushed her, pointing to a boy who must have thought no one could see him holding his sweetheart's hand under the table. The girl then pursed her lips together and made kissing sounds. Most of the group laughed, but one boy had the decency to scold, "Don't be so mean."

That's what a good friend would do. Someone like Aiko who had told her just last night, "I know he's a good boy. Henry didn't mean any harm. And nothing happened." Hanako raised her head, nodding to an elderly woman she didn't know well except when crossing paths in the lavatories. In their old store, she'd been polite and patient to her customers.

The old lady gave her a small dip with her chin and continued on past to another table where each female was busy with a vest, taking their turn and sewing their one French knot in red thread. The other women gestured "come over," and Hanako pointed to herself, mouthing "Me?" She gathered Henry to go join them. Some young man, she learned, had enlisted. He was going to fight to prove his allegiance to the United States. His mother had painted a tiger on lightweight white cotton for his senninbari. How soon, Hanako wondered, before he would be shipped out to boot camp at Camp Shelby.

One Issei woman pulled Henry close. "If only they stay this young."

Hanako narrowed her eyes, pressing her lips together. She watched as the boy sighed, allowing the woman to pat him on the head.

"No worry," another said in Japanese. "Tiger always return home."

But everyone there already knew that wasn't true. When the vest was passed to Hanako, she looped the thread twice around the sewing needle, piercing the cloth to draw the red through. "Almost finished," she told the others, pointing to her knot in the lowest row.

"Saa," they murmured as a group. "You, nine hundred fifty-six knot." Then they started looking around the room for any other female stragglers to wave over.

Hanako sighed. They had her knot; they didn't need her anymore. To be polite, she told Henry to wave good-bye.

II.

Today, she and her son were going to the library—a walk past the hospital and administrative buildings. There weren't that many books but maybe she would reread her favorites. First, they would stop at the canteen to see if anything new had come in. Her husband, Shinzo, badly needed new razor blades. Hanako wouldn't let him grow a beard.

"You don't want to look bimbo," she'd lectured him. But Hanako had had to agree when Shinzo threw up his hands and told her in whispered Japanese that everyone in camp already looked poor and broken down. The whisper wasn't necessary since everyone could hear through the barrack walls, their voices rising through the knotholes and the spaces in the ceiling where the walls didn't meet. Twice every day, she swept their quarters but the wind kept blowing dust inside through the uneven boards and leaving little piles in the corners next to the pot belly stove. Even wetting the floor down didn't help. Still, Hanako felt that their family needed to maintain appearances. They had been shopkeepers only two years ago. She gave her husband credit though, at least, for spending more time with Henry. Yesterday, the two had gone swimming in the waterhole to cool down. The summer's temperatures were well into the nineties. And Henry's older brother who worked as mechanic in the camp's auto repair was teaching him how to change a tire. Hanako knew her son and daughter-in-law were fighting about whether or not enlisting into the army was a good idea. His pregnant wife kept her mouth shut when it came to Henry. And there was her own teenage daughter Lillian, who was too busy with boys and dances and the Hi-Jinx Club. She'd been the most dramatic, refusing to be seen in the same room at the same time as "that boy." Lillian always waited fifteen minutes after Henry left their room before going out.

Hanako guided Henry past their barrack row towards the main road where the washrooms and lavatories stood. She'd made sure to wear a scarf around her neck—something she could cover her head with against the heat or block the wind that suddenly kicked up the dirt. It was a long walk. Along the way, Hanako noted again how hard it was to tell any of the apartments apart. Some families had put up planks with their names carved into them. "Good for us to walk," she told her son. "And maybe we can find a better cook in a different mess hall. One that might have otskemono and rice every day." She'd heard this rumor, but no one had actually found such a place.

Hanako drilled Henry from an old homework assignment. The paper was worn at the creases where it was folded into quarters. What is eleven plus forty-three? What is thirteen minus four? Sometimes Henry would stop to draw the numbers in the sand to see the problem before he answered. She wanted to keep his mind busy. This way, Hanako thought, Henry wouldn't have a chance to ask embarrassing questions she couldn't answer.

They passed a lone man sitting among the sagebrush, reading a letter. They passed families on the steps of their apartments and two men carrying a large plank from a wood pile. They passed people with both hands gripping sloshing buckets of water for their victory gardens.

At least the further away they walked, there would be less chance of knowing someone. On these trips, Hanako hoped maybe she could find another boy Henry's age who would play with him. A stranger who knew nothing about a little boy, some girls, and the root cellar.

Hanako shaded her eyes, scanning the way ahead. Someone had told her that there were twenty blocks, twenty block managers who reported to administration. That was a lot of people at Heart Mountain and everyone had a set of two ears and one busy mouth.

III.

How fast did it take for news to spread, Hanako wondered as she walked. With the sun directly overhead, she and Henry had almost no shadow. The Heart Mountain newspaper had reported that everyone should be aware of rattlesnakes. Henry said that he had seen one under the porch at school. He'd been careful, so he had said, hands behind his back, as he edged further away while some firemen volunteers pinned its head before killing it with shovels. "It didn't rattle," Henry said.

Hanako's thoughts drifted. What else could she tell her son? The Allies had invaded Normandy on June 6th. Everyone knew that almost as soon as it had happened—bulletins had come from the hakujins who ran the camp. But General Eisenhower hadn't said where the troops had landed. They couldn't hear President Roosevelt's speech because radios weren't allowed. People had to guess what was going on. They learned only later the landing took place in Normandy, France. Hanako reasoned, old rumors only died when they were replaced by juicier or more up-to-the-minute news, especially when every day seemed the same.

The air felt hot on her face. It had felt hot on the day when the three mothers had marched their three daughters up to her apartment steps. Later, she bit her knuckle whenever she overheard others talking. How had she heard it? It had been old Otani-san who had described the group as swinging their arms as if marching. The children were being herded before them like chicks. She imagined dust clouds rising up with every step of the group like the way thunderheads roiled up in the sky.

It had been that summer hour after dinner. She'd been sitting on her cot, using the waning light to let out the trouser hems of Henry's pants. The boy was growing so quickly. Her door had been open to let out some of the heat.

Her silver needle kept slipping between her fingers. Hanako had felt the sweat from her scalp run down the back of her neck. Already, her seven-year-old stood up height-high to her shoulder. She had pushed her damp bangs out of her face with the back of her hand, hair falling out of the knotted bun she'd put up that morning. Maybe she should wear pants like some of the other women who'd decided the heat was better than being bitten by horseflies and mosquitoes. Still, it didn't seem right. She'd heard the other Issei women gossiping about baggy bottoms, shaking their heads at the sight of frayed suspenders or even worse, the patch sewn right at the seat of one's rear end.

It shouldn't matter, Hanako told herself, what one looked like. How could anyone be neat and clean in Heart Mountain. The latrines and laundry rooms were often out of hot water. Their G.I. issued clothing and catalog orders made everyone look alike. Right after the last mail drop, she'd seen the same button-down blouse with small flowers on a fellow Issei lady, a teenager, and a stocky new mother.

"Mrs. Ku-ni-to-mi," one of the woman had called, stretching the name out. She called the name two more times, her voice becoming more strident.

The heat had made Hanako slow. The sun was behind the barrack. As she walked out, she found the steps and front door in shadow. Maybe they didn't see her, she thought, counting six people. It was too hot and there weren't enough stools or chairs to seat everyone. There was nothing Hanako could offer to drink. A part of her was annoyed by this sudden intrusion. What could they want? There had been no polite "good evening."

Still, Hanako had clasped her hands together and made a small bow. "What brings you to see me?"

One of the women motioned to one of the little girls, gesturing her forward. Round-faced, her short hair parted down the middle, the child backed herself into her mother's skirt.

Another beckoned the leader, "Think of what people might say. We should tell her inside, not out here where everyone can hear."

Hanako had stood against the door as everyone funneled inside. She thought the extra heat from six more bodies made the room even stuffier and hotter. No one sat down.

"Tell her what you told me," one of the mothers spoke to her daughter. "I'm Mrs. Yamada," she said, turning to Hanako. "This is Ruby." She gave the girl a little push forward.

Ruby glanced over her shoulder, then eyed the other little girls. "Can't we go home?"

That's when a different child in a blue cotton dress began talking slowly. "We were playing with our dolls, make-believe in houses with pretend children. Henry was hanging around. After a while, he asked us, if you're the mommies, where are the fathers?" She rubbed her hands up and down her arms.

Hanako could hear the creak of the floor boards as the other women shifted their weight from foot to foot. She thought about asking everyone to sit down again. She noticed one woman study Henry's cot with his rubber ball and jacks, then quickly glance away.

Ruby coughed. "I asked Henry if he wanted to play daddy to my dolly. He shrugged and asked what can they do. Daddies, I told him, can drive the car. They can go to work." Ruby turned to face Hanako. "Henry told me, not here in this place. That's what he said. And I said, yes they do. Mine works at the fire station."

The girl in the blue dress added: "And mine works for the farmer with beets. Then Henry said, not if they're old. Not if they're Japanese-Japanese from old Japan like my father. I have to call him Otosan."

Hanako felt Mrs. Suyama's eyes staring at her. Why were these women making a small story seem so important? These three were young mothers in their twenties. Henry had been a surprise pregnancy when she should have been done with babies. She was probably the oldest in the room.

The third girl finally spoke up. "And we said oh. I call my father, Pa. My doll's dress had a streak of dirt because she'd been busy sweeping. I unbuttoned the dress and took it off her. I was going to shake it out."

The girl in the blue dress said quickly, "Henry kept looking at the doll."

Hanako felt her skin grow cold—as if her body couldn't take the heat anymore and turned off. She saw all the mothers glance from their daughters to stare at her. It felt like the tips of arrows notched and aimed at her head.

"Go on," said Mrs. Yamada.

Ruby took a breath, her voice growing quieter. "Henry said he knew a secret. Want to know where babies come from?" Her voice sped up. "We followed him into the root cellar. He lined us up against the barn wall inside." Ruby's head nodded towards the third girl. "Minnie got scared. He told us to take our panties off. Minnie ran away."

Hanako leaned her back against the wall. The rough wood felt hot; the sun seemed to blast all the way through. But it was better than the clamminess of her sweat. "And what did *you* do?"

Ruby tilted her head, glancing up at her mother, then back to the other girls. "He didn't see anything under my skirt. Not my bare parts, you know. It was so hot. I took my panties off. We just stared at them on the floor. Nobody kncw what to do next."

Mrs. Yamada ran one hand over her sweaty brow. "Good thing, that's when the workers came in. They were there for more crates."

Hanako had closed her eyes, but the red darkness didn't erase anything. When she opened them, the three girls and their mothers were still in the room. "But nothing happened," she said, surprised that her voice wasn't louder than a whisper. Hanako forced air in through her nostrils. "He didn't touch you. He didn't do anything."

It must have been Minnie's mother who spoke. Hanako wasn't certain. All she heard was, *"What kind of mother lets her son do these things?"*

Wasn't she doing all she could? Couldn't people see that?

Suddenly the wind began kicking up the dust. A small pebble struck the back of Hanako's hand. She rubbed the reddened spot. Then, she became aware that Henry was shouting.

"Over there! Mama!"

She didn't know what her son was pointing at. But the air felt heavy; she seemed to be swathed in the heat. Before her, Hanako saw only the mass of rock that was Heart Mountain—the one break in an otherwise flat landscape.

IV.

The wind was beginning to build so quickly, she hadn't noticed when it started. On the horizon, its black tail anchored to the dry brown land, a funnel tilted from side to side. What had begun as a brief tickle in air so warm, her head seemed to float until she realized that the cowlick on the back of Henry's head was bobbing up and down. The flag on the pole, its grommets and snap hooks, its lanyard all bumped together in a muted clang.

The whole day, Hanako's voice had been like a leash—soft when Henry was near her, shriller and sharper the closer he came to other people. One old-timer with a straw hat started to give them a wave but ended up clamping his hands on the brim to keep it from flying away. Dust devils began dancing in the road; sagebrush rolled on by. Clouds of sand billowed up.

In the distance, dark spots scattered apart. Hanako shaded her eyes with one hand, squinting. She had made a triangle out of her scarf, tying two ends into a knot under her chin. Henry was holding a handkerchief to his mouth and nose. The wind was growing so strong, Hanako wondered if it might blow Henry away. Those who could disappeared inside their barracks.

Hanako skirted the side of a building, gesturing to Henry. But the boy was staring at something in the distance: three dark blurs. Onc dot was larger as it darted in and out of the shade of the barracks. First Hanako saw the dust clouds kicked up by shoes when at first she thought the shape was a small boy. But the long hair flying behind made Hanako realize it was a young girl in pants. The closer she came, the more Hanako felt a weight inside her grow.

Out of breath, the girl bent over—doubled, bracing her hands on her knees. Henry ran up to her. Whatever words were spoken were blown away before Hanako could hear. Everything was being blown away. It was Ruby who put one hand out against the wind. Straightening, she pointed at the two dots behind: her mother with the arm of an older woman draped across her shoulders, hobbling slowly forward. A strong gust blew from behind Hanako, pressing like a hot hand against her back. She watched as the old woman stumbled and fell, struggling to rise with Mrs. Yamada's help.

The wind was howling now, pushing sagebrush into rolling wheels. The older woman kept trying to close the front of her dress with one hand. Long white tendrils of hair tangled wildly around her face. How badly had the older woman fallen, Hanako wondered, as the couple came closer. She could feel the sand filling her shoes and she could barely stand up herself. Had the old lady been struck by a flying tree branch? Now Hanako could see the long cut on the woman's forehead oozing blood.

V.

It had been Henry's sharp eyes and idea. A truck had been parked next to the flag pole. The cab could fit two people. They had laid the old woman down inside, her head in Hanako's lap.

She could see the hospital, maybe a half mile away. It was hard to tell. Henry, she knew, was a strong boy and Ruby had quickly recovered her breath. Mrs. Yamada, she thought, was stouter, younger, stronger. "Go," Hanako repeated, shooing them with her hands. "I take care."

Despite her fingers putting pressure on the cut on the forehead, she saw the handkerchief slowly redden. Hanako swore she could feel the lump become a knot as the flesh continued to swell. How, Hanako tried to ask, had this happened?

Three or four buttons were missing from the front of the old woman's dress, and her hands kept trying to pull the two sides closed. Hanako frowned as she glimpsed the white brassiere peeking through. She thought she must be maybe ten years younger than her patient. The age spots on their arms were the same. When the woman spoke, all Hanako received were garbled, half-Japanese answers about why were so many bells ringing. How her head hurt!

"Wind storm," Hanako tried to explain, but all she saw was widening, confused eyes as the truck rocked with another strong gust.

"Ahh," the old woman moaned, shaking her head. Blood smeared across her forehead, beneath the square of cotton.

Hanako frowned. What could she say? She didn't know Mrs. Yamada's first name and here they were, two women in a beat-up truck. "You're hurt," Hanako said in Japanese. "A cut on your head. Ruby went for help." She lifted the handkerchief up slightly to see how badly the cut was still bleeding. The air in the truck was stifling, the heat and weight on her lap growing more uncomfortable. She waved her hand in front of her face when a sheet from somebody's clothesline slapped into the windshield, making Hanako jump. It blocked her sight, caught for a moment on the wipers before flapping away like a ghost.

The old lady batted her arms weakly, fingers whacking the rearview mirror and grazing Hanako's chin.

"Wind storm outside," Hanako tried again as she caught one arm with her free hand, pressing to the wound with the other. "We're in truck. Stay still. Help come soon."

But the eyes of the old lady grew bigger yet. Her slack-jawed mouth rasped for air. "Itai. Itai. Itai," the woman kept moaning. Bucking her hips, she tried to pull her skirt down past her knees. "Touchan, nooo," the old lady sobbed, the "o" sound becoming a long moan.

Hanako held the thin shoulders down. "Stay still," Hanako spoke loudly to be heard above the wind, her voice growing rough as she turned the bloodied handkerchief to a cleaner side.

Tears leaked from the old woman's eyes, following the trail of crow's feet.

Hanako froze. Why was this woman crying out against her father? A man, who no doubt died long ago. Had she been beaten? Hanako felt her eyebrows raise up into a peak. Had Mrs. Yamada's mother been . . . forced?

Hanako's vision blurred. She tried to swallow but her throat was too dry. Hanako drew the scarf from around her neck and carefully wrapped it around the woman's head over the handkerchief. Stroking the right cheek with the back of her fingers, she tried to whisper: "Daijoubu desu"—what her own mother had whispered to her when she was young, what she had told her own children. But how could things be fine?

VI.

Hanako was altering an extra-large peacoat for Shinzo. She'd done two others to make a little money. Despite the heat of the summer, everyone remembered how cold it had been last year. Though the administration had given them the coats, nothing fit. It was still a lot of work, but she was understanding the job better. Maybe she could do something with the trimmed-off bits of wool. Nobody wasted anything. The work went best when she used a makeshift seam ripper and cut the coat into its parts: sleeves, yoke, collar. She was teaching Aiko to do the same for her two teenaged boys. As mothers, they wanted their families warm when winter came. She was so busy now, she didn't care that Mrs. Yamada had never said thank you.

Once the Nisei doctor had opened the car door and swept the old lady up, she was no longer Hanako's responsibility. Still, Hanako had been curious and followed everyone to the hospital just to make sure. Who knew that more lay ahead?

Henry had eagerly watched the orderly give mouth-to-mouth resuscitation, to see Ruby's grandmother's cheeks slowly pink after that ghastly pale complexion. Hanako wondered about the sight of the young man's lips over the old woman's mouth, the sounds he made blowing air into her lungs. The sight had given her embarrassing thoughts. Later, the doctor had made a butter-fly bandage, using gauze and alcohol to clean the head wound.

Hanako dutifully reported the old lady complaining of a ring-ing in her ears and not knowing that they were in Heart Moun-tain. The doctor had listened carefully, making notes on a chart.

Henry said that Ruby wasn't allowed to talk to him, but that he often saw her standing outside the hospital. Ruby would yell encouraging words to her grandmother when the old lady could sit by the window. Then when no one was watching, Ruby would give him a shy wave of her hand.

But Ruby and the girls she hung around with didn't matter anymore. Henry had tried out for peewee baseball and made left outfielder. Most of the men were talking about the swing Henry had made with the bat that had sent the ball flying onto the barracks' rooftops. Who'd think a seven-year-old had that much power? Now much of Henry's time was spent practicing how to catch fly balls. Shinzo had grown a beard, seeming to spend many morning hours grooming it with a special comb. Their crowd of acquaintances had changed.

Hanako didn't even mind that her scarf had never been returned. It would have been blood-stained anyway. Poor Mrs. Yamada, she often thought, when she saw her in the mess hall. Everyone had talked about how the mother wasn't and would probably never be right in the head, walking around the hospital halls like someone lost.

She'd told her good friend Aiko what she had seen. The way the old woman had tried to cover herself, pulling her skirt down. Nobody knew anything for sure. It was obvious to her, but Hanako asked her friend anyway. "Touchan," Hanako said, letting a small silence hang between them. "Who you think that might be?"

"Nickname for father, probably," Aiko had answered with a look.

Hanako nodded. Through her one small window, she could see the mountain cutting into the blue sky, the sun a bright disk glaring down. "Be careful," Hanako warned. She could tell that Aiko was getting rough with the peacoat's wool. "One stitch at a time. You don't want to make holes."

Vindaloo

Hank Teraoka looked around the Indian restaurant filled with the smells of curry. He felt uncomfortable in the dark room, sitting next to the curtained window and fingering the one-page plastic menu. He couldn't help but catch glimpses of heavy brows, the cook's black eyes staring from the kitchen, at him—a Japanese man in his eighties. Hank didn't understand anything on the menu. Not the luncheon special—Shahi Korma? But it was cheap, a plate lunch for only $7.95 with something called basmati rice, which to his mind should be Calrose or Nikko sticky white rice.

He had asked for the corner table where the light was brightest, where he and Teru had sat only nine months ago. Even then, he felt the two of them had been out of place—his wife's Seattle Mariners sweatshirt zipped up tight against the cold. They had stopped at this restaurant because they'd always passed it on their way home from her kidney dialysis session. The background music with its lazy beat and quivery stringed instruments hadn't mattered then.

Hank lay the menu down against the bright orange tablecloth, picked up the water goblet and took a sip. He half expected to see his wife's short white hair, the weight of her head tipping her chin down and making her look sleepy. Everything without Teru was a first time.

The technicians at Day Vista Dialysis Center had hugged him, patting his back, when he brought the four boxes of Hawaii's Best chocolate-covered macadamia nuts. "For taking such good care of my wife," he had whispered, hoping his voice didn't sound shaky—too emotional. At least there would be no more needles, no more tubes with dark red blood flowing in and out of the fistula in Teru's left arm. She had never sat still, wanting to hurry up and go home. So many times when the technicians had been busy, he stood in, applying pressure with gauze squares to stop the bleeding. His fingers had grown stiff, their joints getting stuck. Finished for the day, she had always been hungry.

"We have to try something new," Teru had told him. Hank could tell by the sound of her voice that *we* meant *you*. He'd always been happy with a nice steak and green onions dipped into a small mound of salt. "So bad," she used to shake her head at him. "No wonder you have high blood pressure."

The dialysis people had told her, no tomatoes! Eat lots of vegetables and protein. And after Teru's last session, they had stopped at the strip mall. Here, where they saw the sign: Cedars Restaurant. Right now, it bothered Hank—why couldn't he remember her order? All he could think of was that the lunch had been something green.

And then the waiter was by Hank's side, a white sleeve stained with a swipe of yellow. What he wanted was Teru's special teriyaki sauce, a meaty drumstick that Hank could dig his teeth into. He wanted the familiar ketchup taste with sugar and shoyu. Teru hadn't made anything good since she started the dialysis treatments every Monday, Wednesday, and Friday. She said it was easier to eat out. Teru had liked letting the menu be a surprise. Once she had ordered crepes wrapped in lettuce with a shallow dipping dish on the side filled with an oily-looking vinaigrette. They had been at a Vietnamese restaurant. Bending forward, she had murmured: "Ooo, that looks different!" But Hank was always looking for something he could recognize: beef, chicken, fish.

The waiter, trying to be patient, clutched his order pad; the stubby pencil was poised to write. Hank had been sitting for at least fifteen minutes, and there were a dozen tables with business suits and student backpacks to wait on during the lunch rush.

"This," Hank said, finally pointing at random.

"Vindaloo?" the waiter asked.

Hank nodded his head vigorously to keep from mispronouncing the word. At least there had been pictures at the Thai place. With Teru, he had tried Jamaican, Greek, and Creole. "Where do you want to go next," he had groaned. At home, alone now, all he had to look forward to was a can of Vienna sausages or deviled ham.

Steam rose from the tray the waiter carried to his table. As the bowl was placed in front of him, Hank felt the spices sting his sinuses as he inhaled garlic and chili. Even his eyes teared up, and he had to dab at his nose with the paper napkin. Blinking hard, Hank picked up the spoon, waiting a moment to stare at the chicken and potatoes swimming in a brown liquid. Teru always said, the first taste was the strangest, the most unfamiliar. Hank gulped the red wine and vinegar broth down. He could feel the heat slowly travel past his tongue, the back of his throat. He could feel the slow burn along his esophagus. It reached into his chest. Nodding his head, Hank took a second bite. This mouthful was the same as a lot of other new foods he had eaten. He'd be able to manage finishing about half a portion. But that didn't mean he had to like it.

Sworn

Monte sat knee-close to his mother in the waiting room. He didn't want anyone to think he was skipping school, when he should be memorizing fractions and long division. Small for twelve years, he knew that most people thought it strange to see him buying groceries with a five-dollar bill; or clipping a lawn's borders with sharp-pointed shears in too-big overalls, the straps falling off his shoulders. Hunched down in his chair, Monte wondered how else he might take advantage of being small.

Okasan cleared her throat; Monte knew she needed him. He'd have at least two chapters to catch up on for the arithmetic test scheduled tomorrow, but her smile made Monte feel important—he was doing more than helping around the house. Speaking English for her was something only he could do.

Across from him, an old man with a cane propped up against a chair arm was reading a magazine with a yellow border and the words "Sports Illustrated." There was an advertisement of a blond woman in shorts on the hood of a pickup truck. The old man lifted his head just enough to see over the edge of the cover, then back down again. He coughed, a phlegm-like sound, and swallowed.

Monte's mother, her back straight and purse resting carefully in her lap, gestured toward the table with other magazines. Right now, she didn't look bad. Her face was flushed, almost rosy. Okasan probably wanted to look at the pictures of food, at what white people ate—not the yellow takuwan served up at dinner with their rice, or the miso-drenched mackerel. Monte knew she was ashamed of her broken accent mixed with Japanese. The "Redbook" was probably a good bet. Curling the pages back from the spine, Monte tapped his finger at a roasted turkey. Potatoes along with onions and beets were presented on the same plate. "This looks good," he told her.

"Sato imo?" his mother asked. "Okii desu, neh?"

Monte shrugged one shoulder, then scratched at his head. He really wished his father wouldn't cut his hair so short. The Idaho and Russets weren't anything like the fuzzy Japanese vegetables served up. Boiled, they were a kind of gray in color. But as far as Monte knew, they were still potatoes. "Yeah, they're big ones," he finally answered, his hands mimicking the size.

"Not from around here," the old man spoke from behind his magazine.

Monte wondered if he should say anything back. He hadn't exactly been asked a question and he wasn't sure if the man was talking about potatoes or that his mother was speaking Japanese. Okasan nervously shifted in her chair to get Monte's attention. She nodded in the old man's direction. It would be best, Monte thought, if she didn't say anything more so he held up his index finger to his lips.

That's when the receptionist called out their name: Momo-hara. Monte could feel the old man staring at them as he and his mother rose and walked to the front desk. "Which one of you is Miho?" the woman said, looking first at Monte and then at his mother. Okasan's black hair was done up with soft curls that bounced on her shoulders. Monte didn't understand why she would dress up for the doctor. Okasan seemed to think that anytime she stepped out of the house, she should look her best—"to put her best foot forward" was how she'd explained it in Japanese.

Monte was proud of the fact that in the print dress she was

wearing, his mother was an attractive woman. Okasan's face was oval and pale, the jet black of her eyebrows emphasizing the tilt of her eyes. So many of the housewives who lived in their same apartment building were overweight. If they wore any kind of lipstick, it was a bright red smear that looked like a wound. Today, Okasan's belt was pulled tight to hide how big her dress had grown, the weight she'd lost. Okasan knew enough to smile, to look people in the eye and nod her head even when she didn't know the right answers. But then most kids Monte knew could do that much. Now came the hard part, the explanations. "She is," he said, dropping his voice to a distinct whisper. He knew how his mother felt, not wanting to be embarrassed, about not knowing what she was being asked to do. Monte stood up, pulling his shoulders back as he added: "She needs me to tell the doctor what's wrong."

While he spoke, Okasan lifted her eyebrows, turning her head to follow the conversation—from the receptionist back to Monte. She kept her arms straight, her hands clutching her purse, nodding vigorously, saying "Yes, yes, yes." Monte winced at the way his mother's tongue lingered on the S sounds, wishing the answer had been timed just a little bit better. Okasan had rushed the cue.

The receptionist tapped her pencil against her front teeth. Monte knew what she was thinking. He was a boy, after all, even if he was small. "Tell you what," the woman spoke slowly, directing her comments to Monte's mother. "I'll let the doctor know you're here, and then the three of you can work it out in the examining room."

Half an hour later, Monte led his mother down the hall and through a door into a small room. There was only one chair; closed venetian blinds shut out the view to the other six-storied buildings on the same block. The counter was lined with glass canisters full of cotton swabs, tongue depressor sticks, and gauze. Monte almost put his hand down on the clean examining table that was more like a bent-in-the-middle blue vinyl chair, covered in a long sheet of thin tissue paper. A swing-out table and strange spurs were connected to the bottom.

Okasan kept looking at the examining table until Monte made her sit in the chair. He took her purse for safekeeping and because she was starting to weave on her feet. She was hurting, maybe even more than before. Her palms straightened the skirt of her dress, but the thin arms kept coming back up to wrap themselves against her stomach.

"You'll be okay," Monte told her. It felt weird to say the same thing his teacher would tell him. Mrs. Littlefield could tell when he studied hard. It didn't always happen. He remembered the time the class had struggled through double-digit division and he'd been the only student who had raised his hand with the correct answer. "The doctor will help," Monte continued. He didn't know what else to say but he felt responsible, needing to take charge. Monte figured at least he knew more than his father who only came home to sleep and then went back off to work.

Almost six weeks of his mother lying in bed had passed, where she kept asking for only a little more rest before she got "bettah." Six weeks of Monte making the same peanut butter sandwich for his lunch, of cooking rice for his father's dinner. If anything, Okasan looked even weaker. It was hard to do school-work, in addition to doing all the dishes, and vacuuming the house. Lately, Monte hadn't even been able to do his homework. Okasan had to be coaxed to drink even a little miso soup, always wanting her cooling hot water bottle changed. Monte looked at the walls when his mother didn't answer. Gently, with cautious little pats, he stroked her shoulder. "Anata wa, *good boy* desu," she answered.

Monte knew she appreciated him, so much more than the mothers of all the other boys in his school. At lunch time, he'd heard them all complaining about not being able to stay up late or not buying them the latest three-speed bicycles. He understood when the other boys talked about their moms wanting them to stay home, messing with their hair and clothes, complaining about cleaning up their rooms. Okasan said the same kind of stuff, but he was different. He had to take care of her.

There were hanging charts, cut-away pictures that showed the outline of a woman's chest—the layers of respiratory, digestive, and circulatory systems. All of it reminded Monte of the cut-out dresses he'd seen little girls make, collars and puffy sleeves laid over and hiding a cardboard doll's neck or arms. Tabs held everything in place. Monte turned away, not wanting to stare at the outlined nipple of one diagram's breast.

To make Okasan feel better, Monte talked to her about how the bus driver hadn't charged him full fare to go to the free clinic. That meant he'd saved them money. He still had to figure out what the doctor might ask. Looking at the steel examining table, he wondered if there might even be a physical exam. Monte remembered Clara Worthington, the British girl in his class. She was epileptic and had had a seizure during recess once. "No, it didn't hurt," she'd told him on the playground, her fingers curled against the cyclone fence as she rocked back and forth. Clara said her parents had her checked out; specialists had fitted wires to her head and watched lines made by a machine jerk up and down.

Monte tried to explain to his mother that she might have to remove her clothes. Okasan might have to wear a special gown and let the doctor put the stethoscope on her chest. She didn't like that and got all guzu-guzu. Why, his mother wanted to know, couldn't Monte just tell the doctor her symptoms? Couldn't they just give her some pills to make things better? Monte shrugged his shoulders; neither of them had ever been to a hospital before.

Most of the time, Monte thought he understood what his mother was trying to say. It wasn't the words exactly, more like her tone of voice and how she repeated certain things. His mother was like Barbara Stanwyck, playing out a part. She was always wanting to see American movies. She didn't act like other mothers, like Jack's ma who had a restaurant and made Jack help carry out platters of steamed rice and sukiyaki on a big round tray or clean up tables. Jack's ma was rough, always in a hurry, her face red from the hot kitchen, from working to feed Jack and his six other brothers and sisters. Or Yosh's mom, who worked sewing factory dress pieces all day for Dolly Madison Company. Yosh's mom wore wire-frame glasses because of all the close needlework. A long time ago, after Monte had started school, Okasan had once tried to work the ACME Poultry chicken line but she hadn't lasted more than a day. She'd come home with her right hand swollen twice its size. Her job, from what Monte could make out, was to pull out chicken guts on an assembly line. Monte's father had shaken his head and Okasan had gone back to taking care of the house.

What had his mother really been saying, Monte wondered. Was she lonely, or regretting that all the hard work and late hours his father put in as a janitor and fry cook never added up to a better apartment? Come to think of it, Monte couldn't remember the last time he'd seen both of his parents in the same room. Since his mother became ill, his father had taken to sleeping on their living room couch in his shorts and sleeveless T-shirt— loud snores rasping the night. Sometimes, Monte could hear him muttering loudly under his breath. Monte knew his father was worried about money. Sometimes he'd complain that if Okasan's English was understandable, maybe she could get a job as a maid. More sons and daughters could have helped the family out. There had been babies before, Monte knew. But he only remembered the time his parents had told him he was going to have a baby brother or sister. His father had strutted around the neighborhood with his mother at his side, sometimes patting her stomach. But something had gone wrong. Okasan's belly had gone from being bloated to skinny. Mrs. Ishii, who knew stuff about birthing babies, had come over, but Okasan had never gone to the hospital. She'd cried a lot, but neither of his parents had said anything. A few neighbors had asked how was she doing, but Monte was careful: "The same," he'd tell them. "Everything's fine." He knew enough not to say anything that might make the family look bad. Or pitiable.

When the doctor came in, Monte was surprised to see a man the same age as his mother, dressed in a white lab coat, a pen clipped to a shirt pocket next to the name Larry Truscott, M.D. Seeing Okasan wring her hands, Monte felt himself straighten. It was up to him to make certain the doctor understood. "Kasan," Monte started. "She doesn't understand English very well." Then Monte thought about how that sounded. "But she's taking lessons," he quickly added.

Dr. Truscott smiled at Okasan, then held his hand out to Monte to shake. The doctor's fingers felt clean and warm. He didn't even smell like antiseptic. Monte wondered if the doctor would make some comment about missing school. But instead he said, "Responsible boy, aren't you." We got lucky, Monte thought, watching Dr. Truscott open a file folder: "There's some things I need to know about you, Mrs. Momohara."

Every time the doctor asked a question, Monte noticed, he'd first nod at Okasan—waiting to see what she would say. When Okasan looked blank or embarrassed, Dr. Truscott would turn to Monte. Monte started to interrupt, like he'd seen his father do, to answer the questions before his mother had a chance to look down at her feet. But the doctor would hold up a finger to stop him, pause—observing the looks between Monte and his mother, making sure Mrs. Momohara had a chance to elaborate.

It was like being in class, Monte figured. This had rules: You had to raise your hand to be called on, you had to wait your turn.

In the beginning, the information was easy—like the first day of school when the teacher read all the names off the roster. His mother was born in Yokohama. Okasan married, left Japan, and resettled in Seattle. This year, 1940, she had turned thirty-two years old. Okasan sometimes nodded as she recognized key words that Monte gave, the doctor jotting down notes on a chart.

The trouble began when Dr. Truscott asked, "What are your symptoms?"

Monte took a deep breath. How could he say anything about the late nights when he'd stare through the crack of their tiny apartment's bathroom door. His mother had sat on the toilet, her nightgown hiked up to her hips. She'd been doubled over, moaning, the small tinkle of urine striking the water. He remembered how he'd wanted to look away, torn with wanting to help and saying nothing.

Monte massaged the back of his neck. He didn't want to stare into the doctor's eyes to reveal his mother's secrets. "It's her tummy that hurts," he said slowly. Then he reluctantly added: "She's in the bathroom all the time."

It was too shameful even for his mother to tell him, her son—worse than the bloody toilet paper that didn't always flush down. How could he embarrass her even more? There were certain things a boy wasn't supposed to know about his own mother. His cheeks burned just thinking about it. Besides, the only Japanese words he had were "benjo" and "shishi"—silly baby words one used with family, but not in polite company.

When Dr. Truscott spoke, his voice seemed overly loud as he asked: "Can you show me?"

Monte's mother lowered her chin, turning away. Hesitantly, she stood up. The man pressed Okasan's stomach, right under her belt. Okasan held her hands out to the sides above her waist, wincing as he explored lower down her groin. "Itai, itai," she moaned.

"I'm sorry it hurts," Dr. Truscott said.

Outside, rain was beading up on the windows. The sky was a metal gray. Monte could hear the honking cars amongst the downtown traffic. There were some things that Monte didn't have to translate.

Okasan seemed to know what was going to happen. She didn't want to, but Monte and the doctor had said over and over: The hospital needed tests to make the pain go away.

Back in the waiting room, Monte thought about how Dr. Truscott had escorted him to the door, how this important educated man had told him: "You did the right thing to make sure your mother came in."

Monte held his mother's purse in his lap. He could see his shiny silhouette in its patent leather reflection. After today, Okasan would gain weight. Maybe she'd even find a job. Maybe Monte could learn and study hard enough to become a doctor. But then again, it wasn't a good idea to boast. People might think you were a know-it-all. Even when you worked hard for something, when you waited. Everything good that had ever happened to him made others unhappy. If he got good marks, the other kids in his class called him a teacher's pet while his father expected more. If he made a little tip money from doing an extra good job cutting lawns, he was supposed to share his wages. Like the special treat of soda pop, Monte tried to hold the fizziness on the tip of his tongue for as long as he could. He'd learned to hold his little moments inside himself.

He'd have to work hard to catch up for this one day of missed school, of errands. Was it worth it? Okasan had pulled on Monte's sleeve—she who so seldom touched him or his father. Then she had pointed to the door once the nurse had come in. Maybe she knew she had to be brave? The starched white uniform seemed stiff with sharp creases across the lap, around the waist and inside the elbows.

Sitting and waiting was hard. Monte checked the round black and white clock for the fourth time. At school, about now he'd be hiding out at recess, trying to finish his homework. His rushed penciled answers usually held the imprint of the bumpy ground he wrote on.

The old white man walked slowly as he returned to the waiting area, the rubber tip of his cane softly thumping in time with his steps. He stopped once and checked the zipper on his pants. "Had to pee twice since I've been waiting here," he announced to the receptionist. All of the other chairs were open, but he lowered himself into the seat next to Monte. "You still waiting on your mother?" he said. The man's breath smelled sour. Monte didn't want to answer. "Did you hear me?" The man spoke louder, "Little boy like you shouldn't be in a doctor's office."

Monte slowly nodded his head. Mrs. Littlefield, his teacher, sometimes acted the same way. Adults talked about all sorts of things that didn't always make sense. Most people just wanted someone to agree with them. Then they'd let you alone. Monte slid deeper into his chair, wishing he could disappear.

"I'm supposed to be next. Stupid receptionist told me I had to wait just to get a doctor to look at my cough. At least there's cool air conditioning here." The white man pulled out a crumpled handkerchief, frowned at it, then put it back in his trouser pocket.

Monte rustled his magazine and pretended to read. Suddenly, it became important to learn the recipe to prepare a turkey with bread crumbs and stuff it with gizzard meats. He hoped the nurse would call the old man's name soon, but she was busy on the telephone.

Five claw-like fingers gripped Monte's knee. "She and that doctor are taking too damn long." His grip grew tight, but not enough to hurt. Monte tried to brush the hand away, but the man's face was leaning in close. Monte could see the dark age spot riding on his forehead. A gleam came into the old man's eyes. "Pretty woman, your ma," he said, pursing his lips and winking. "Kind of small, though." It wasn't a good wink because both eyes fluttered before the right one closed shut.

Monte tried to shift his leg away. A few older boys at school sometimes snickered and whispered behind the gym as they snuck puffs on a cigarette. He always avoided them, but even at a distance he could hear them shout dirty words at him— practicing their "god damn bastards" and "screw yous"— laughing as he hurried away. Once he'd asked Yosh, who'd spent three summers on a farm, what "screw" meant. "You know," Yosh had boasted as if glad he knew something Monte didn't, "... how you make babies."

The old man hadn't used any of these words, but the way he leered—Monte knew it meant the same thing. He pushed the hand off his knee and half-ran to the receptionist's desk. "I just remembered something," he said. "I should tell the doctor."

When Monte glanced back, the old man was pointing a finger at him.

As Monte inched open the door, all he could see was the wide white back of Dr. Truscott's lab coat. What he'd planned to say was that when his mother got scared, she'd pretend everything was normal. He didn't want the doctor to get the wrong information. He wanted to make double sure what Okasan said was right.

The doctor seemed to think the interruption was the nurse with syringes and vials because when he stood and swiveled, his eyes opened wide above the mask across his face. Dr. Truscott tried to hide a steel tube with pinchers. It was his mother's voice that drew Monte's attention to the examining table.

The neck of Okasan's white gown was straining against the two small mounds of her cleavage. A paper-like blanket with damp smudges was spread across her lap. Her knees were open and spread apart. Swatches of gauze and petroleum jelly lay on a separate metal tray. "No," she moaned softly as if crying out but trying to keep the sound in, one arm shielding her face, her right hand trying to hide her crotch.

It was as if Monte could feel the pressure building inside, the throbbing red balloon of his mother blaming herself. There was nothing he could do. What could he do to help? Dr. Truscott had seemed like a good man. But even with plastic gloves on, even in his white lab coat and narrow tie, it still wasn't right for anyone to touch Okasan's bared belly button, to see the ridges of her hip bones, to hear the fine high keen of her shame.

He wanted to strike out at Dr. Truscott with his fists. He wanted to beat the man, hug those black-clad knees until they buckled and brought the weight of him to the ground. He wanted to comfort his mother, cover her, but he was afraid of her touch, of what he had seen. The best Monte could do was turn his back, to stagger two steps out the door and prop himself against the wall, slowly sliding to the floor.

Harsh fluorescent light lit the hall. His was the only shadow, a cut-out stretching from the soles of his sneakers. Something felt lodged in his chest. English? Japanese? Monte had no breath to speak.

Slippage

Always, her mother had praised Warren. As a bank manager, he was too important to reschedule meetings. And Martha had been the one left to scold and take away the takuwan, the fermented tofu, the soy sauce and sit by her mother's side as the technicians at Day Vista Dialysis plugged in the tubes to the shunt in the withered arm. Only one good spot left, a doctor had told her, for a transfusion line. They should save it for later. That "later" never came.

Mostly, she talked to Warren on the phone. His distant voice had insisted: "Don't worry about paying the hospital. Ma has plenty of money."

Plenty, Martha had thought as she imagined her brother holding the cell phone, his other hand covering his ear like he always did.

She shrugged and studied the front door with its dead bolt and chain. The house was almost empty. Little trace of her mother remained. Stacked next to the front door were boxes and overstuffed plastic bags for her younger brother to go through. Things like locks with metal keys, things like the Coleman ice box and gallon water jug the family had used for camping. Martha had found them in the back of the basement closet. She'd sorted through the clothing, toys, and furniture for what was still usable, like the card table with a wobbly leg. Family possessions she couldn't make herself let go of but didn't want for herself. She'd lugged the last of four folding chairs towards the pile, propping it up against the wall. Martha could still hear her mother saying, "When you go to the basement, think about what you can bring back up." Trip after trip: downstairs with boxes, upstairs with the junk to be thrown out. Was it a Japanese thing? she wondered. Martha stopped to catch her breath.

Warren was always late. Sometime in the afternoon, he'd said. It was past three o'clock. Warren didn't have many weekends off. Martha didn't see him much except for Thanksgiving and Christmas and their father's memorial, then those long days at the hospital, and finally with the hospice nurse at home. Martha knew Warren had hired a gardener to mow the lawn. He paid the bills and balanced the checkbook. Her mother had always brightened at his two kids, opening her arms for hugs and kisses on her cheek. Whenever Warren and his family were around, it had seemed like they pushed Martha out of the room, to clear away the makizushi and oden that Ma had taught her to make. For her to gather the dirty dishes for the kitchen sink because Martha knew her mother didn't have the strength to wash them. To be fair, Warren's wife always offered to help. But Ma would shift the conversation, insisting "sit, sit." Ma had said once to Martha in private, "What do I know about the kinds of food Warren and the kids eat?"

Divorced. No babies. But Martha had a steady administrative assistant job at Providence Hospital. She owned her condominium and liked to travel with her girlfriends from her book club, once bringing her mother a wool shawl from Ireland. "Itchy," Ma had complained, rubbing her arms. Martha enjoyed ocean cruises, meeting strangers who became her ocean family for a week as they walked around on the slippery deck to glimpse the blow hole plumes of whales.

Martha saw herself as a responsible child. She'd gently bathed her mother, careful not to bring out the purple bruises so quick to pool under the papery skin, and laundered the soiled sheets.

Towards the end, she'd slept in her old twin bed in her room across from her parents, listening for the bell she'd set on her mother's night table. Finally, Martha had been the one to lay her fingers against the cold cheek, then her palm against her mother's chest, to tell those gathered by the bedside: "No breath. No heartbeat."

Warren had invested in Microsoft. He and his wife had a two-story house in Bellevue with a view of Puget Sound. He had never offered advice about her own nest egg. "You have to be willing to lose money," he'd once told her in passing, before their mother had called him out of the room. And Martha hadn't brought the subject up again. She was the type to hoard every penny, keeping coffee cans full of change. It had always been her way. Even with her babysitting jobs, Martha had put aside a little to give her parents, especially after her father was laid off from his airplane wiring job at Boeing during the recession when everyone was leaving Seattle. There had been that famous billboard sign on Pacific Highway South—*Will the last person leaving Seattle—turn out the lights*. Martha could see Warren loosening the neck of his white shirt with his index finger. "The house needs fixing before we put it on the market," she'd told him. "Leaky kitchen faucet. The toilet runs. I can call a plumber."

"Nah," Warren had answered. "I can do it."

"You need to pick up your stuff," she'd added. But Martha didn't know if he'd heard before the dial tone hummed in her ear. She couldn't remember if Warren was good with a wrench or if her brother had watched their father work with duct tape, tinkering around the house trying to save money.

As the son, Warren was the executor of their parents' will. He knew numbers, but so did she. After high school, she lived at home, taking a stock job at Nordstrom's bargain basement shoe department while attending community college. It was less expensive to transfer after her A.A. degree. Martha bit her tongue as she thought again of how her mother had gone through her jewelry box, giving Warren the diamond ring and wedding band to pass on to his own daughter. Or the used Chevy Impala Warren got, for his good grades and transportation to an out-of-state college. Pressing her lips together, she nodded, breathing heavily through both nostrils.

Martha walked into her old bedroom, the one place that had been hers—the one with the pear tree shading the window. The walls were blue. In third grade, Martha had stayed home from school with the measles and a high fever. She hadn't recognized her mother, thinking Ma had been a bothersome Warren, whom she told to go away, leave her alone, slipping herself deeper until the blankets closed over her head. Alone, she had stared at the walls and imagined a sea tide rising and falling away. Voices warbled around her like water gurgling in her ears, flowing over her neck as she floated on her back. Bound by her twisted nightgown, she'd tasted something bitter that spread from her tongue to the sides of her dry mouth. Every part of her had itched as she burned. How she had rubbed and scratched herself. She'd been convinced that when she'd opened her eyes, her fever had shot out like lasers. Touched by her swollen fingers, her body heat had melted the walls into textured swirls. No one else had noticed. No, her mother had insisted, the walls were exactly the same. No one had believed. But to this day, small white scars remained on her abdomen. Martha fanned her face with a hand; why was it so warm?

She pulled a crumpled piece of paper from her flannel shirt pocket and checked her list. Almost everything was crossed out, except for the few small tasks Warren had promised to take care of. Martha moved on to the living room. The hard wood flooded with shadows as Martha closed the venetian blinds. She didn't want strangers peering in from the street. She didn't want them to see how empty the house had become. The realtor had told her that the large lot with its fruit trees, its location only three blocks away from an elementary school—these would help with the sale. When her parents had purchased the house for $14,000 back in 1958, there had been three other Japanese families on the block along with a retired couple and a widowed teacher. Judy Sumiye, from across the street, had been her best friend.

Did Warren know how to fix things? Martha glanced at the wall phone still in its old spot at the end of the large kitchen. Here was the door jamb that measured their growth, the door jamb Martha had fallen and cracked her forehead against. The gash required a butterfly bandage. Warren had lived downstairs in the basement past their father's shovels and tools, past the canned foods her mother shelved for emergencies, past the hot water heater and noisy furnace. Warren had secrets in his room like the dried blood from his nosebleeds he rubbed against the wall until their father made him wash it clean with bleach and hot water. And the *Playboy* and *Hustler* magazines he hid under the mattress.

Why had Warren wanted to come home at all? Martha wondered if there was a special floor board with something else he had hidden away. A long time ago, when they were kids, Warren with his first pocket knife had cut clods of dirt out of the backyard's lawn to make small holes for a cache of cats'-eye marbles, a skate key, a shiny match box. "You need a treasure map," she'd told him: "Five steps straight out from the left corner of the patio, turn right and take three more steps . . . like that." Three weeks later, forgotten, the holes were overgrown with grass.

When Warren came through the front door, she was surprised to see him in jeans and a grey sweatshirt. For a moment, he looked like any kid brother coming home from playing basketball with his friends. Except for the gray threading through his dark hair, except for that thickening waist. Then there was the red toolbox which Warren placed on the floor. Martha stared, slowly realizing it was her father's. When had he taken that?

Warren's jaw dropped when he saw the stacked boxes. He groaned, "More stuff."

And I Goodwilled most of it, all on my own, Martha thought. "There's your train set with the steel tracks, even some of those smoke pills for the chimney. Your comic books: *Fantastic Four.* Your carp flag for Boy's Day." She remembered how she'd been jealous of some of her brother's stuff. Ma and Pa, they'd always found a way to give Warren what he'd asked for. She was the eldest, the one who would find a way to do without.

Warren said, glancing away: "I want to get started on that kitchen faucet."

Martha snorted. He was the one who had taken the entire morning and afternoon getting here. Her brother turned the worn spigots on and off. Did he really know what he was doing? Martha frowned as Warren wiped his fingers on his pant legs. The stainless steel was dirty because she'd been running only a small slip of water to keep the drain from backing up.

"It's probably been years of rice and grease," her brother said. "I'm going to have to wrestle the basket strainer out."

He's saying it's my fault, Martha thought. I didn't run the hot water often enough. I let Ma flush down coffee grounds. She stooped to pick up a hammer.

Warren raised his eyebrows and reached past her for a pipe wrench and needle-nose pliers. "I want to fix things, not make them worse."

Martha felt her face flush. Warren shouldn't complain. Everything under the sink, she'd chucked into the garbage: old coffee cans, never used-up bottles of detergent, moldy pieces of soap. Still, she shook her head as Warren scooted his way under on his back, muttering about the lack of space, how hard it was to work with all the pipes and nuts and washers above him. That was his problem, she decided. Dutifully, she tried to hold the flashlight's beam steady.

"I need to put some torque on this nut," Warren said, breathing heavily. "Hold the pliers here, like that. Got it?"

Martha wasn't sure what she was doing. It was crowded and hot and she didn't want to touch her brother or get in his way. She just tried to stay still and to hold the one position he'd assigned her. That's why she wasn't prepared when Warren gave the pipe wrench a hard jerk and the pliers flew out of her hands. The propped-up flashlight rolled, rattling across the kitchen floor.

Warren's head thudded against the bottom of the sink. "Baka," he yelled.

She hadn't heard the word in such a long time. Idiot. Stupid fool. Their father had used the curse when he was angry, when things weren't going his way. The word was like a bomb going off and then Pa had given everyone the silent treatment, the rooms of the house echoing with his heavy footsteps. Like when he glared at another house payment bill. If he lowered his voice and spoke the word slowly, somehow it was even worse. "Not you," her mother had tried once to explain. "Pa means himself."

"Let's forget this whole thing," Martha said. Inside her head, she felt like she was shouting.

Her brother paused as if counting to ten. From the dark under the kitchen sink, he said: "I thought you were ready."

"I'm too old for this," Martha replied, struggling to her feet. She felt a small twang give in her thigh as she picked up the flashlight. "Why waste effort?"

"Because I can do it," Warren said, his voice muffled, even softer. "Don't you remember how the whole family changed the light socket in the basement? There was Pa, trying to save money, standing on that white stool Ma used for cutting hair. Pa was teetering back and forth, his arms wind-milling for balance. Ma told me she was afraid he'd fall, or worse, electrocute himself. She held his legs to steady him. Sometimes, Pa would put his hand on her head or shoulder when he got tired. I held the flashlight, trying to aim it at the right spot but there'd always be a shadow that got in the way."

Martha shook her head. She didn't remember anything like what her brother was describing. "What did I do?" She checked the flashlight, turning it off and on again, pointing the beam under the sink until a circle of light found Warren's face. He held spread fingers up to block the glare. No wonder Warren's voice sounded funny. He was lying on his back, head pushed against the back wall as far as it could go. Martha aimed the light back on the pipes.

"You read the instructions he'd written down from the hardware store," Warren answered. "You tried to be so clear. Ground wires, red wires, pig tails, nuts . . . I thought we were all going to die together when Pa put the light bulb in and told me to flip the switch." He sighed. "And it worked."

Why wasn't that event anything close to what she knew? Martha wondered. She wanted to tell Warren to come out from under the sink. She wanted to correct her little brother with the facts. Ma had held the flashlight, and it was the washing machine they'd been fixing while their father had struggled with putting on a new belt. She'd been reading from the manual. It was like that one time she'd emptied her savings account to pay Warren's spring quarter tuition. Warren had never said thank you. He hadn't even asked where the money came from. But he'd had that lousy job as part of a clean-up crew for Super 6 motels and Kentucky Fried Chicken while studying statistics and business law at Lewis and Clark College. Now that she thought about it, maybe her parents had never told her brother the money was from her.

Warren shifted his position, one knee pointing towards the ceiling as if to give him better support. "One more time," he said.

"What exactly do you want me to do?" Martha wished she had more hands as she tried to understand her brother's instructions.

In the end, fixing the sink didn't take as long as she expected. Maybe it felt long because she had been holding her breath. Tools were scattered across the linoleum floor with its checkered red and white squares. An old bucket was half full with dirty water, and her mother's old and holey dish towels were soaking up the puddles. Martha had kept them for the final clean-up. She wasn't ready to say good-bye to the house just yet. At least the sink was fixed. She was afraid to mention the toilet.

Warren wiped beads of sweat and grime off his forehead with his sleeve. Licking his lips, he opened the door of the refrigerator, saw nothing, closed it, then opened it again. Cool air flooded into the kitchen.

"Don't waste money," Martha almost said, mimicking her mother. Why was Ma's voice so loud in her head? Especially here. In her own condo, Martha never said things like that. Instead, she murmured, "There should be a couple of cans of pop in there."

Warren handed her a drink, then snapped the tab of his own. He leaned against the stove counter, then turned to open and close the storage cabinets. Taking a swig from his Pepsi, he said: "Ma kept the good stuff, the canned eel, on the top shelf. And the dried shrimp. Those cans of Vienna sausage and deviled ham."

A lot of the cans were years past their expiration date. Did Warren want them? There was something about the way her brother's hands clung to the cabinet knobs, his arms spread wide apart. If she were a girl again, jumping up to peer over Warren's shoulder, she'd imagine the same things. "Kuromame," Martha broke in. "They were always too sweet. Disgusting black beans. But everyone had to have at least one mouthful . . ."

Warren finished the well-worn refrain: "to have good health for the new year." He smiled, nodding to himself. "I didn't chew. You know, I just swallowed them down. Your problem was you kept chasing them around on your plate."

Maybe he won't remember about the bathroom, Martha decided. Her can of pop was cold in her hand. She could almost hear Pa saying that toilets were easier than sinks. Straightening her back to ease the kink in her shoulders, she took a step towards the oven and the four burners. The kitchen table was gone, but she could still see everyone seated while her mother dished out steaming rice into their ochawans. From the way his nose twitched, Martha could tell that her brother was remembering yet another kind of food.

"I miss those carbonated tablets, those Fizzies. Jungle Juice. Ame Candy. Dried fish jerky that was salty and sweet." Warren shyly smiled. "It was surumi. Ma passed it over the front seat during car rides on the way to mushroom hunting."

He could be that boy again, Martha thought, the one who balance-walked the length of fallen giant fir trees at Mount Rainier. That's how she saw him. She wondered about asking if Ma had fed his kids wasabi peas. She wondered if they knew any Japanese. But they probably didn't. She'd taken two years in high school. Her instructor had commented on her calligraphy brush strokes—"pretty healthy looking"—as he tried to be kind. When she thought about it, most of her Japanese came from the food her mother prepared. Maybe five hundred of those words were left. It was here, in the kitchen, where they came back. One of her cruise friends had told her, if you didn't speak French every day, it slipped away.

Martha pressed her lips together and swallowed. Slowly, she gathered the wrench and pliers, fitting them back in the red tool box. On her hands and knees, she mopped the floor with another clean rag while Warren took out the garbage. Light motes hung, twirling like small undiscovered moons in the thin afternoon light. Looking up, it was as if a shadowy figure stood at the fixed kitchen sink, as if running the cold water and looking out the curtainless window towards the T-shaped clothesline and the apple tree behind it. Was it memory, or Ma's ghost? This was the last time she and her brother would be in this house together. She looked around the kitchen and noticed that the sunset changed the pale blue of the walls. Only Warren was left.

.

Stealing Home

Jojo lets loose a piercing whistle, rocking back and forth on his perch and flapping his green wings as I kick my two overstuffed suitcases into the living room. My parakeet probably heard the key turn in the lock despite the radio playing to keep him company. Barry Manilow hits every high note of the chorus, wailing "...you *caaame* and you *gaaave* without *taaak*ing..."

Bags full of last-minute souvenirs drop onto the sofa. My back is aching from the flight and shuttle bus home. Seven days in Peoria, Arizona, for spring training, and I never got a glimpse of any Mariner worth a damn: no Ichiro Suzuki, not even Joe Pineiro. I'm such a sucker.

What sounds good is a hot shower and eight solid hours of sleep in my own bed. The Motel 6 I stayed in had sheets so rough, my skin is still itching. My one-week vacation is over. Tomorrow, at 6:00 a.m., I'll be driving my bus through downtown traffic.

The house is stuffy with the smell of bird droppings. I open the windows and sliding glass door, turning Manilow off before I get to Jojo. Maybe it's because I've been gone so long. What's to miss: the green leather sofa, the coffee table with its watermarks from my beer bottles, the aluminum foil clamped onto the television antenna? There's something about the living room that feels different, something other than an unhappy green parakeet. As I wiggle my finger through the wires of his cage to offer a head rub, Jojo pecks hard, drawing blood. "Goddamn bird," I yell, spilling his tray and scattering seed onto the already messy rug. Jojo and I are flat-out pissed off at each other.

I rinse my finger under the kitchen faucet, certain I'd left a coffee mug and cereal bowl soaking. But the sink shines, as if someone had taken a sponge and Dutch cleanser to it. Jojo continues to scream, his voice rising in a series of insistent squawks. Water drips all over the linoleum floor because I can't find the dish towel I usually keep on the refrigerator door. My dusty tennis shoes leave muddy skid marks.

When I see a large bottle of no-salt shoyu and five packages of Top Ramen—all lined up next to the toaster—that's when I finally realize Ma's been here. Tightly wrapping the edge of my T-shirt around the bleeding, I remember that I'd stopped the newspaper and mail. Since Ma kept harping on helping, I'd tried to keep things simple for a seventy-four-year-old lady. All I'd asked was for her to do was to check my parakeet's food and water. Once on Wednesday was good enough. I'm her youngest boy, the one with no wife or girlfriend, the one who drives a bus for the city. Now that I know she's been here, I coo to Jojo: "What are you trying to tell me? What did that crazy Japanese lady do?"

After all that squawking, Jojo can't wait to get at his clean water. Jojo arches his neck as the liquid dribbles down his throat. Ma has a hard time thinking of a bird as a pet. I can hear her lecture: "Birds should be free to fly, not caged all the time." But what she means is that she wants to brag about something other than Jojo when it comes to me.

Finally, I flop down on the sofa for a few seconds' rest. I'm so tired and my eyes are full of grit. I rub them hard.

When they clear, I study the four walls of the living room. There's a lighter, cleaner rectangle of paint next to the front door, the spot I pass by at least twice a day. My back teeth grind, and my breath explodes through my nose. The only thing I own that gives my house a little bit of class is missing.

It's an old picture, in a 24 x 20-inch gold frame. A muscular tiger prowls through a black-and-white jungle, its stripes rolling across his shoulders and flanks. It's the tiger picture that my parents had in the living room where I grew up, what Dad gave me when I finalized the loan for my thirty-year mortgage. Paul, you're grown up now, Dad said; you have a house of your own. A tiger in a house means good fortune. You could use this more than your mother and me. This tiger is now for you, for your future, for good luck.

At first, I check the kitchen and bedroom. Maybe the picture fell down and Ma stacked it up against a wall until I could fix it. But it's a useless search. Nothing could have made this day worse. I feel totally betrayed by more than the Mariners. I can't believe my own mother would steal something out of my home.

Even though I have a key, I ring the doorbell. My brother Frank and I are always telling our mother, it doesn't hurt for her to be careful. Just last month, the manager found some homeless guy wandering through the halls on the third floor. Frank made certain that Ma got a two-bedroom apartment with a view of the park here at the Kawabe House, an assisted living place that caters to Japanese-Americans. On the nights she doesn't cook for me, Ma eats in the dining room, joining the other gossipy seniors.

As I wait for the door to open—balancing a bottle of apple jelly in one hand, peach preserves in the other—there's that weird sensation I get of being examined by a single eye through the peep hole, of being studied from the far end of a telescope.

The moment I step into the apartment, my mother asks: "What's wrong with that bird of yours? Squawk, squawk, squawk!"

There's no "hello" or "how was your trip, Paul," to start our conversation, no pleasantries. She goes on, complaining about

Jojo's vocabulary, how I've taught him phrases like "batter up" and "My, oh my." Ma's voice is big for such a small woman. "Parakeet or no," she insists, "he was a green mess of feathers, hanging upside down like a bat." Ma taps one finger against the side of her head. "Crazy."

Is my mother referring to Jojo or me? Obviously, she doesn't mean herself. My puzzlement must show on my face or the fact that it's taking me so long to answer. Ma makes a low sound in her throat, exploding with an "aah, you!"

In the ride up in the elevator, I went over my strategy. Though I was lacking actual proof, no one else could possibly have been in my house. But if the tiger picture was in her apartment, I could catch my mother red-handed. "What's this?" I could play-act, maybe even being nice enough to let her off the hook a little. "You probably wanted to surprise me by getting this reframed."

More than anything else, what I want is an apology. But Ma's the same silver-haired woman I had dinner with two weeks earlier. Today, she's wearing an oversized Hard Rock sweatshirt with "Las Vegas" in gold block letters.

I hand off my bottles of apple jelly and peach preserves, my way of officially thanking my mother for checking in on Jojo. I know she'll probably "re-gift" them to her friends, but I didn't know what else to get. She has everything she could possibly want. "That's just what parakeets do. It's normal," I mutter, even though I know my answer is too late. For a moment, I wonder why we never hug or kiss each other's cheek. Ma's always affectionate with Todd and Ronnie, Frank's boys.

Then it occurs to me that I have a witness. Jojo probably saw my mother remove the picture off the wall and carry it out in a paper grocery bag. In fact, that's what I should be looking for.

In an attempt to change the subject, I point at the windows and ask, "New curtains?" Of course I'm spying, but I don't want to seem obvious. There are the usual pictures of my older brother

Frank, his wife and two sons on the buffet next to a huge stack of large-print *Reader's Digests*. All the way from Japan, a three-panel screen of long-legged cranes stepping in and out of a lake graces one wall. The framed glossy of my dad sits on its own special shelf with a fresh bouquet of black-eyed daisies. He seems to be resigned to wearing a suit and tie, when in real life he wore flannel shirts even on the hottest days of summer.

Ma pretends she doesn't hear me. I can tell by the way she glanced at the window before returning to the kitchen. She's more selective in her old age, avoiding questions she thinks are too tiresome to answer. White rice is cooking in a pot on the stove. She's already chopped up her nappa. Tofu, clear noodles, sukiyaki meat—everything is ready; it just all needs to come together. She turns on the electric burner under a beat-up skillet.

As she stands next to the stove, wooden spoon in hand, I'm tempted to tell my mother all about the lousy work days I've had since I've been back from Peoria—about the SUV that wouldn't let me merge onto the freeway, the middle-aged lady driver who gave me the finger. Or the smart-ass high school kids who piled on at the shopping mall, two of whom conveniently "forgot to pay." It's as if all the hard luck in my day-to-day life has busted through the spot on the wall where that picture hung, like the one rock holding everything back. But I don't say anything about my job or vacation.

Instead, I double-check her savings account and pay bills on her dining room table crowded with a paper napkin holder, trivets, and plastic place settings. That's how I know what's going on in her life—how she's donated twenty-five dollars to the Nisei Veterans Sukiyaki Dinner, or that she took a day trip with the Jefferson Community Center to see the Bloedel Reserve on Bainbridge Island. This winter, she's taking a basket-weaving class for seniors.

Ma chatters as she cooks, about how Mr. Yanagihara is losing it, how nobody invites him into their rooms anymore. He just can't be trusted. He thinks everything—mugs, umbrellas, raincoats—are his. Alzheimer's, she says, stirring the vegetables with a wooden spoon in disgust. Ma shakes her head, tsk-tsking the poor man in the next.

I stop a moment from licking envelopes, from trying to follow her round-about logic. There was a time when Ma punched out our last name, Uyeda, on one of those label makers, sticking the bright red strips on the bottom of every material object she decided was important. That way, if someone took it, she'd be able to reclaim it. Of course, whatever the family owned was community property—like when I was five years old, having caught her holding my piggy bank upside down. A butter knife helped guide the coins out of the slot on its back. "We need bread," she told me, the knife jiggling more furiously, "for your school lunches."

As we eat dinner, our chopsticks dangle noodles between mouthfuls of rice. Ma finishes a swallow, then announces: "I took back the tiger to give to Frank."

The seats aren't bad for Opening Day when hordes of fans swamp Safeco Field. I'm surprised to see the sun shining for the last day of March. Still, I tuck my hands into my armpits. I can't depend on enthusiasm to keep me warm throughout nine innings.

Frank shouts at the boys, Todd and Ronnie: "You guys have had two hotdogs and enough peanuts to stuff an elephant. That's enough. Pay attention to the game." My older brother is shelling out plenty of bucks for this male-bonding experience. Frank and I have never gone to movies together, or even had the same friends. Ma must have said something to him about "being an older brother" and "what's good for the family." Other than him having a guilty conscience or wanting to smooth things over between the three of us, I can't imagine a reason for this sudden generosity. It's a good thing Frank is a District Manager for Fidelity Investments.

The four of us Uyeda men sit without speaking until it's the Raiders turn to bat. All around us, fans are chattering. It's a reversal of this loud quiet that I feel churning inside of me. "You had no right," I had yelled at my mother. My waving hands had knocked over my tea cup. I remember how she had stared at the puddle spreading into the tablecloth, almost flinching in surprise. What had happened to Paul, the pushover?

All these years, I had been making excuses to myself as I spent entire weekends driving her to different shopping malls in search of a "special gift" for the boys' birthdays. How many ugly spinster daughters did I take to the annual church bazaar because I had "nothing better to do"? My voice had been guttural, the words like an avalanche of rocks spilling down a cliff: "You can't take back something you gave away. That picture is mine. I want it back."

Ma had hunched her shoulders as if she'd been struck. But it didn't matter; I was the one who'd been seriously wronged. Still, she managed to turn her chin up to answer: "That would hurt Frank's feelings."

But what I feel doesn't matter, I wanted to say. Somehow, I managed to keep my feet on the floor. I had both hands braced at the edge of the table.

Ma continued on in a whiny tone: "You don't treat it right. All dusty on the wall. All that good tiger luck going down the drain. Besides, Frank's the oldest."

That's when I had pushed back my chair, grabbed up my jacket, and walked out the door without bothering to close it. I haven't spoken to my mother since. Even though the phone rings twelve, thirteen times, I know who it is. I won't answer.

I crack a few shells, popping the salty handful of peanuts into my mouth. Last year, the Mariners were ranked second in the Western Division. Tickets are expensive. I know when I'm being bribed, but the chance of any promotions other than overtime at Metro is non-existent. I'm a bachelor on a fixed income. I figure I might as well get the most out of the situation. Frank was smart and rich enough to move his wife and kids to Bellevue. Close, Ma would say, to his banking office. *Smart*, her squinchy little eyes always seemed to echo behind her wire-framed glasses, each time I had asked her news about my older brother. Ma always made sure I knew how Frank's wife, a nice local girl, invited her to stay on weekends and that "Grandma" was picked up to attend her grandsons' judo exhibitions and debates.

Together the crowd cheers, the Mariner Moose running in front of the dugout, when Felix Hernandez throws out a pitch against Oakland. I was really looking for Ichiro Suzuki to strut his stuff. Slowly, my nephews start to wiggle in the hard seats, standing up deliberately to stomp the peanut shells under their tennis shoes. Bored with pointing out the fans with blue paint on their faces, Ronnie starts egging his brother on. "Gimme your hand," Ronnie commands. Across the small palm, he traces a curving line, explaining, "This is a truck on the highway. But it has an oil leak." Ronnie lifts his brother's hand up close to his nose. "Smell it?" I scowl as Ronnie shoves Todd's hand into his face.

I'm lucky that Frank never acted like Ronnie when we were kids. At least, Frank was never that blatant. All through high school, teachers would shake their heads at me and complain: "*You're* Frank Uyeda's little brother?" But it was the stuff he and Ma said, how it was too bad I never got much time to actually play short stop for my high school baseball team. It was "really nice" that I even made the team, but I had to remember to keep my grades up. Stuff like that made me feel like a loser. "Hey, Ron," I smile and give him my middle finger. "You're a real little shit."

Ronnie looks at me and just smiles, a cheesy grin spreading across his round face. Todd shrinks down into his seat, feet kicking back and forth. A younger brother like me, Todd is suddenly quiet, like he knows something is wrong.

"Really adult," Frank says, wrestling my arm down and trying to hide the obscene gesture. But I twist away, shoving both of my hands deep inside my jacket pockets. "How long are you going to give Ma the silent treatment?" Frank starts to lecture. "Jesus, Paul—how long are you going to act like a spoiled little kid who can't get his way?" The batter pops a fly ball into Ichiro's left field. It's an easy out. I keep my eyes on the pitcher's mound, trying to see if there are any signals to the coach.

Frank looks a lot like my mom, especially the eyes that disappear into slits when they smile. The kids do, too. They all have round faces, little button noses, and the straight black hair that tends to look greasy. I'm the one exception in our family who took after my father. At least I'm taller than my older brother. That and the mustache I grew make me different from them. It's always been this way: Frank and Mom sticking up for each other. Dad and me nodding our heads, saying "sure," and "whatever you want."

Once I got home from Ma's dinner and cooled down a little, I let Jojo out of his cage. My parakeet minced up my arm to settle on my shoulder. I asked my bird if I was being too hard. The softness of his feathers brushed my chin as he turned around, inching back down to my hand. I stood in front of the missing picture. It's funny how I could see those flowing stripes of the artist's tiger, the huge head turned with the ears lying flat, mouth opened. The black lines of the lip make the canines stand out, the tongue lolling, one paw raised to take the next step. The artist had used a gold silk for his canvas, and brush strokes in black ink. Tigers, I learned from PBS's *Nova*, have stripes that go all the way down to the skin.

Frank doesn't really care about baseball at all, so he doesn't see the Oakland player on first base. We're in the bottom of the fifth, and the Mariners should have been more attentive. I'm uneasy about the runner because he's already a good three shuffles off when Felix Hernandez goes to the plate.

Whole rows of fans jump to their feet, me included, as we boo the steal to second base. My brother Frank is completely clueless. "What happened?" he stutters. Ronnie and Todd jump up and down, trying to see because suddenly they're surrounded by a forest of adult legs.

An older, barrel-round fan tilts back his baseball cap, telling me: "That should never have gone down. Not in the majors."

I nod in agreement, dropping more shells and chewing another handful of peanuts. It's only a second base gain, but this isn't what we fans wanted to see. Good professional athletes shouldn't need this kind of edge, unfair to catchers and infielders. I'm hoping Frank doesn't embarrass me with one of his know-it-all comments. Of course, my brother has to add his two cents: "But it's legit, right? It's a tactic, a perfectly acceptable game play."

Ronnie watches his father's face, following the discussion between me and the old-timer. "Aren't the Mariners winning?" he asks.

Frank tousles Ronnie's hair until cowlicks are sticking up at all angles. I can tell my brother is trying to impress his sons. "Maybe they'd be in *first place* of this division," Frank winks at his son, "if they used Oakland's strategies."

Everything to Frank is about how he can make himself look good. He's the better son because he has connections and an upper management, high paying job. He made sure Mom was taken care of after our father died, splurging for a full-out reception for the memorial. Frank's boys will make sure there are plenty more Uyedas in the future.

I stoop down to one knee in front of Ronnie and Todd so I can be eye-level. My index finger scolds the air in front of them. "You two can be just like your Dad," I tell them. "Little chips off the old block."

My big brother raises his hands to shove me off-balance. Suddenly, I'm sitting on my ass, on the cold cement of the bleachers, legs sprawled in the aisle. Frank looks down at me. Mouth partly open, a strand of spit slides down his lower lip. "All because you can't get what you want," he mutters. A coat sleeve wipes the red face dry. "Paul," he says and pauses. When Frank says my name, there's a finality to it. Like he's never going to say it again. Then he adds, "There's no way in hell you're ever getting that picture back."

On the way home from Safeco Field, traffic is backed up for miles. Here I am, hands hanging onto the steering wheel the way Jojo's feet cling to the cage bars. Trapped behind a semitruck, my Mazda inches forward. Of course I can't see anything in front of me, nothing except Safeway's insignia—a skinny red "S" that looks like a yin–yang sign. For thirty minutes, I read and re-read their slogan: *Ingredients for Life*.

Right now, red is my color. It's in the brake lights of cars stopping and starting. My face in the rear-view mirror is red with frustration. That Safeway "S" seems to twist like a red rope.

What good is it being a nice guy? I'm not about to let a Camaro merge into my lane, just to let some macho punk get home five minutes earlier. Barely three inches separate my bumper from the back of the grocery truck. I shouldn't drive mad, but I am. Actually, I'm not driving at all. I'm wasting gasoline, completely stalled. "Ingredients for Life," I repeat to myself. For forty-two years, I've bothered too much about what other people might think. It's what my mother trained me to do.

I can't think of any time Ma has said something nice to me. It's always stuff like "You need a haircut." Or "when is the last time you mowed your front yard." My witty comebacks, those things I should have said, are days too late in the middle of the night. How can I defend myself when she's done such a great job of always making me feel guilty for what I haven't even done yet? Her voice echoes in my head: "Why don't you come visit? Frank does. I'm all by myself, you know."

Putting up with my family deserves compensation. Yin and yang. Tit for tat. If Frank keeps the tiger picture, I should be entitled to something else. There's so much I never even tried to ask for. Because Frank was student body president in high school, he got skiing lessons. Because Frank graduated with honors, the folks bought him a used car.

Logic tells me I've behaved well. Ma doesn't know what a good son I really am; I've had plenty of opportunities to do drugs. I never hung out with the gangs. My clenched fists say I should act now. Frank didn't even dare me to come and get the tiger picture—he's that sure I'd never even try. Ma and Frank, I mumble under my breath. Frank and Ma. Favoritism sucks. But between the two of them, I'm angrier at my mother. She's the one who started this train wreck.

Against the law, I make a U-turn into the oncoming traffic. Several cars hit their horns, but there's no siren or motorcycle cop on my tail. I head for Ma's apartment. I park three blocks away from the Kawabe House.

The white-washed stucco building stands out against the sunset. Red paints the entire west side. Most of the twelve stories are dark, but there are a few lights on here and there. It's a little after 6:00 p.m. and many of the tenants eat their prepared dinners on the main floor. Saturdays, the kitchen usually serves seafood—teriyaki salmon being one of Ma's favorites.

Anyone can come through the main entry's automatic doors. Since I'm Japanese, nobody bothers to ask. In the foyer, I nod at the sweater-vested man who could be my father with the thin strands of white carefully combed over his bald spot. But he's turned away, too blind and hard of hearing to really notice. When the elevator arrives at the main floor, a small group of mummified elders crowd out the door. Several speak a half-English, half-Japanese lingo that I don't understand. One woman with unnaturally jet black hair pushes her friend in a wheelchair towards the dining room. I don't recognize any faces, but it feels like any of them could be my parents. That's when I decide to take the stairs.

I'm a little out of breath, having taken the eight flights up two steps at a time. But I'm also nervous about what I'm about to do. My plan is to sneak into Ma's rooms, then swipe something while she's downstairs eating her dinner. Nobody is in the hallway as I make my way through the building.

The click as the doorknob turns sounds loud to me. It's not even locked. I'm not certain about what I'm going to grab, taking a few moments to think about it. In the quiet of the kitchen, there are my mother's pills for high blood pressure, a bag of potato chips clipped shut, and a newspaper with pages folded back to a sale—all lined up on the counter. Two mangoes ripen in a bowl. I'm surprised because I never knew my mother ate them.

I'm even aware of my tennis shoes brushing the rug, although a part of me is shocked at how easily someone could break and enter. Standing in the middle of the living room, I slowly turn, studying each wall, each possession.

What I take should be worthwhile. Something portable. Nothing like the big-screen television set Ma doesn't know how to program, or the Waterford vase Frank gave her for Christmas. A floor lamp spreads its glow across the sofa with a crocheted afghan draped across the back. Through the curtains, the sunset is still bright against the sky. Gradually, it dawns on me that this is what my mother must see, alone for most days of the year. Frank's touch is there in the Oriental rug and space heater scattered around the room, along with the kid-made artifacts like Ronnie's clay ashtray from kindergarten. I want something I have a rightful claim to.

Dad's picture catches my eye. Ma must really miss him. His frozen face tells me what I'm looking for. Tucked away in her jewelry box is the gold watch Dad inherited from *his* father—the retirement gift from the Great Northern Railway, from working over forty years in the roundhouse. I remember how its solid weight felt in the palm of my hand, the steady ticking sound as the gears wound down. On the polished back are engraved italics: *Susumu Uyeda.*

Ma doesn't wear necklaces—not the gold chains or even the Mikimoto pearls Dad bought her for their twenty-fifth anniversary. She doesn't like pierced ears, and all the bracelets and rings "just get in her way." Maybe she'll discover the missing watch in about five years; she looks into that lacquered black box so seldom.

With long strides, I head for Ma's bedroom. Just at the doorway, I hear snuffling snores, and freeze.

In the dimming light, I can see my mother sprawled out on the queen size bed. She sleeps only on her half of the mattress, one arm spread across the spot where my father's shoulder would be. There's no movement or sign of her stubbornness, only the gentle rise and fall of her chest. In sleep, her face seems gentled. The darkened age spots on her cheek make me realize she's older. Have I ever seen Ma look so helpless? For a long time, I stand there as the light continues to go—taking in the tilt of her head, the spread of her thinning hair, the cupping fingers.

West Coast Blues

Seattle, 1950

I: Riichiro

Riichiro Hikida dipped his mop into the bucket of soapy water, squeezing the ropes of the head through the wringer. He was almost done with the hall; there were just the extra dirty spaces where everyone stood in front of the elevator. He rolled his shoulders to ease his neck muscles. A glance at the clock showed him it was half an hour before his shift as a night janitor ended at 2:00 a.m. Yaeko would be waiting at home, a good wife for thirty-five years now. There'd be the yellow light from the kitchen, her fingers parting the curtains as she peered out towards the road, her head nod and smile of relief.

Locking the back door behind him, Riichiro studied the moon in the night sky. The walk home was all uphill along Jackson Street. The bus didn't run this late, but he saved the ten cents on fare walking to work in downtown Seattle and walking home. He'd learned to toss a six-sided die to decide which of three routes to take to avoid trouble. He knew enough to carry a short sawed-off broom handle in his sleeve resting against the length of his right arm from his wrist to his elbow, ready to slide past the cuff. The thought of actually using it made him afraid.

At sixty-three, he was in good shape. Weeding and harvesting crops in the gardens and farm fields at Minidoka had made him stronger than he'd been as a middle-aged man before relocation. It was hard to believe he and Yaeko had left camp five years ago. Riichiro reached under his open coat to pull up the shoulder straps of his overalls. He'd had other Issei friends who seemed to shrivel up and die, like Shinzo, a bachelor with no future—who'd tied a belt around his throat and hanged himself two days before Minidoka closed for good.

His feet took smaller steps up the incline. Summers in Seattle were the worst, when Riichiro would cross the street and sometimes hide in the dark behind cars if he saw too many people out this late at night. Sometimes the drunks would yell at him to go back to where he came from. He was never quite sure what that meant: if he should return to his work building or if he should continue on home. He knew he didn't belong. It didn't matter; the bums were out of their heads and dizzy with drink. Winters were cold, but everyone was more likely to stay inside and Riichiro made better time getting home.

This spring evening, he was suspicious of the dark Studebaker that slowed down, then sped up to drive past him. A block away, the Black and Tan jazz nightclub doors were still open. He'd walked past the establishment many times before, his eyes caught by the flickering neon sign. Light spilled onto the street. Riichiro thought he would stop inside for a little while, enough time to throw off the car people.

He slowed his pace, noticing a tall black man among the shadows, just inside the alcove to the building. Riichiro bowed his head, standing a few feet away, his hands hanging at his sides. He could feel the broom stick inside his sleeve. "Sir," he asked in a clear voice. "Glass of water, please?" He took a quick look over his shoulder to see if the Studebaker had circled around.

Maybe the man at the door had seen his glance backward. Maybe he'd seen the car cruising up and down the street. Riichiro didn't know why but the man gestured with his forefinger to follow.

There weren't many people seated in the hall. Just the piano player and another musician on a horn were on stage with a singer. The woman wore a dress with a draped neckline. The air was thick with cigarette smoke.

"Over there, in the back," the man from the door pointed. "Someone will come with your water." Then he whispered to Riichiro, "Better for her to have an extra set of ears." He paused when Riichiro didn't answer, and added, spreading his hands out: "You know, a bigger audience."

Riichiro looked around, noticing maybe ten people. He felt like he stuck out as the only Japanese in his shabby coat. Everyone was dressed better in suits and dresses. On weeknights, most Japanese would be home in bed. Just when he was wondering if maybe he'd made a mistake and would have been better off if he'd simply hurried home at a run, a waiter came to place a small napkin and tumbler of water on his table. He nodded his thanks, took two large swallows, then caressed the film of sweat forming on the glass. The man at the piano flexed his fingers and began a run down the keys.

That's when the singer began her song.

Riichiro cocked his head at the music; he couldn't make out any of the lyrics. The singer opened up her mouth wide and tilted her head back to draw out the notes. He could see her dark throat trembling.

II: Yaeko

Rubbing the fabric of her husband's boxer shorts between her fingers, Yaeko knew they wouldn't be dry by morning. The bras, panties, and T-shirts on her laundry drying rack gave the kitchen a damp smell like some rain had blown in.

She put the kettle on for tea. Riichiro would want a light meal. Tonight, she'd made onishime for the two of them—burdock, carrots, potatoes boiled in a dried fish marinade. He'd tell her about his shift or help decide their plans for the week. Then he'd shower and go to bed, maybe sleeping until noon. On the evenings like tonight when she wasn't working for the Seattle Glove company, doing factory piece work, she'd wait up for him. The job was part time and the manager would call her for three or four days in a row, when the orders were busy. Yaeko knew she had fewer hours because she was old and slower, but the lead boss liked the quality of her work, how she would take time to teach newer seamstresses how not to waste effort, money, or fabric. They hadn't called for two weeks now and she was getting worried.

There never seemed to be enough money. Before the war, they'd built up their savings—their two boys should have a good education. Riichiro had run the Pacific Hotel as the manager. They'd had a nice apartment. How quickly she'd seen the numbers in the bank account go down. In camp they had their barracks and canteen food. Issei, the elders, didn't have to work, but that meant no money was coming in either; their wages came to only a few dollars. There were expenses for small things like toothpaste and soap. What people made as farm hands wasn't much. In Seattle, the lease on the hotel expired and Yaeko knew they'd have to start all over. How else were they going to earn money? They weren't farmers and picking fruit was backbreaking work.

Yaeko went to the kitchen window to check for Riichiro's return, parting the curtains for a quick peek. He was later than usual. The moon shone down on the laundry lines, clothespins sticking up every few feet. She shook her head: She could never display such intimate underclothing for everyone to see.

Parallel to the back fence, there were rows of turned earth. If it were late summer, Yaeko could use the vegetables from her garden. Yesler Terrace had back yards for their low-income housing unit. She and Riichiro had been lucky that the Seattle Council of Churches had reached out to their Japanese Congregational

Church. One son and his new wife had lived with them, sleeping in the living room for a year before heading out for better jobs on the East Coast.

It had been different in camp. Everyone was Japanese and they'd had no other choice. Here, the families next door were Italian on one side, black people on the other. The young black woman next door was friendly when they chatted over the fence or sat on their porches.

Yaeko tried to watch out for their neighbor's two children until the parents returned home from work. Once she fed them hot dogs, cut up and marinated in shoyu and ketchup on top of rice with egg. They loved that. But there were times when the children were loud, often running with a stick striking the boards of their picket fence. She and Riichiro were the only quiet ones and it felt like they were in a shrinking shoebox, making themselves quieter and smaller. Who was there to share her feelings with except her husband? She was glad for the church, for the sermons in Japanese.

To keep herself from worrying, Yaeko threaded yarn onto her darning needle and slid Riichiro's sock over an old wooden spoon he had sandpapered down. There were so many patches along the toe and heel but who would notice unless he took his shoes off. Rubbing her eyes with the back of her hand, she blinked at the crowded kitchen. She missed her old furniture: the tansu chest with its many drawers and the low coffee table. Riichiro had told her that their belongings had all been lost. They'd been stored in their church's basement since the evacuation; vandals had torched the building. Only a tiger-on-silk painting and a few plates they had left with the woman who taught them English survived. Maybe that was why Riichiro would go down to Pike Place Market and shop the cheap antique stores on weekends. Was he hoping something of theirs might show up?

Tea was hot and ready when she heard Riichiro's steps on the back porch. Her onishime was warm in its pot on the stove next to the rice. Unlatching the chain and lock, Yaeko murmured as she opened the door: "Saa, osoi—no?" She spoke in the half-Japanese, half-English they had fallen into. After he grunted, she helped her husband out of his coat, careful of the broomstick with its lanyard, and hung them both on the wall hook. She didn't say anything about how he smelled of smoke. She was just glad he was home.

After scrubbing his hands at the faucet, Riichiro sat down with a loud "oof." Then, with his hands holding the cushion seat, he dragged the kitchen chair close to the place setting with its bowl and cup and chopsticks.

As she served up their dinner, Yaeko told him about her day: how she'd used coupons for eggs. The newspaper said there would be a low tide on Saturday mid-morning. About the phone call from their elder son in Chicago. She watched Riichiro chew his mouthfuls slowly and carefully, sipping his tea.

"Eat," he interrupted. "Before your food get cold."

That's when he told her about the car following him up Jackson Street. Yaeko had to cover her mouth with her napkin to keep from exclaiming. A muffled "oh" escaped her when the story got to the Black and Tan jazz club. That's when she asked, "How much you spend?"

"Just water," Riichiro said. Slowly, he held up and spread his index and second fingers. "For two song. Then they close. Nobody outside, and I walk out with the people as they head to their cars. After, I keep walking. Come home." Riichiro smiled and patted her hand where it clutched the table edge.

Yaeko could feel the warmth of his fingers. Maybe it was from the tea but she didn't think so. He'd been walking in the dark so late at night under the crescent moon. It couldn't be helped. He was safe, she reminded herself. When he spoke, his voice had a kind of thrum that filled the kitchen with his presence.

III: Riichiro

Riichiro turned his face into Puget Sound's mist, feeling his boots pull as he squelched through the rocky mudflats. He stood for a minute, watching the tide pull away and scanning the waterline for small holes, dimples, and an occasional squirt. With the sun climbing higher, this afternoon he might see Bainbridge Island or the Olympic Mountains.

The foamy water pulled away, leaving the green anemones to retract their tentacles and become no more than round brown disks stuck to rocks. In the pools, tiny starfish lay hiding on the bottom. With any movement stirring the waters, he could see scuttling baby crabs and fish. They would die if the sun dried out the pool.

Further out, the waves pounded with a distant crushing sound that felt pushed together into one note. The water ebbed, then flowed, circling his boots in shallow water. What had his father told him, that old Japanese proverb? Nana korobi, ya oki. The waves rose and fell, over and over again. "Seven falls, eight getting up," he remembered telling his own children. What he didn't say to anyone was that he was tired. Getting up was harder to do. Better if one was careful and didn't stumble at all.

Riichiro had three more years until retirement. Each afternoon he pushed himself up from his bed, then placed his two feet squarely on the floor. Was it only two nights ago in the shower, when he had tried to quietly decide which bill was more important to pay? Or was a small installment on two or three of them a better strategy? But then the next morning, the phone rang with Yaeko's boss asking her to come work starting on Monday for ten days straight through the weekend. There'd be more pay—a one-time deal. Tonight's dinner would be free clams with leftovers for chowder. Always one more trouble to knock his hopes down, then a reprieve that made Riichiro hope for better times. Smaller things now could be harder, especially when he couldn't do anything about them.

Yaeko was off to his right: a bucket in her left hand, a scarf tied beneath her chin to keep the wind from blowing her hair into a gray-and-white nest. He could see her battle as loose strands plastered her cheeks; she was stopping beside wet barnacled rocks, bending and picking up long sheets of brownish kelp, then holding it stretched out between her hands with the wind blowing from behind her.

They'd taken the early morning bus. Except for another passenger in the front seat across from the bus driver, the interior had been empty. Sitting side-by-side in the back, they'd half-whispered to each other in Japanese. She'd remembered when they had a car, driving with their two sons to the same beach for an outing. Riichiro mostly nodded and grunted. The four of them had a fire on the beach and grilled littlenecks, manilas, and cockles. Fresh off the beach, the briny shellfish had tasted so good.

They wouldn't need as many clams for just two people. Riichiro had decided one bucket full would be their limit, split between the two of them since they were taking the bus and would have to walk home. That and the seaweed Yaeko would wash, cut and dry out in the oven for later. Yaeko had packed their lunches in foil and tied everything up in her cotton furoshiki. That and a small thermos of tea lay next to their hand rakes in the buckets.

Riichiro could feel the sun spread across his shoulders and down his back as he bent and used his rake to dig a shallow trench. As he worked, he hummed softly to himself. Maybe because it was both soothing and sad, he couldn't get the tune out of his head. It wasn't like anything he was used to. The morning was starting to grow hot. At first, each clam rattled the bucket as it struck the bottom. Yaeko joined him, her legs straddled and one hand bunching up the hem of her dress to keep the mud and sea water away. As always, she worked more slowly.

By noon they found a log to sit on not far from the rest rooms and water spigots. A little boy with brown cowlicks and hair parted on the right looked troubled. He wore a striped pullover shirt with pants whose legs were cuffed at the bottom. He circled the restrooms three times, glancing to the left and right down the beach. The boy wiped his arm across his nose, sniffling.

Yaeko cleared her voice and took steps towards the boy. Standing at a distance, she asked gently, "You lost?"

Riichiro watched as the boy's lips began to tremble. The small hands rubbed circles around the pockets of his pants. Riichiro thought the child might run away.

"Come," Yaeko said, half-bending, resting her arms along her thighs.

From where he sat, Riichiro barked, open palm thumping his chest: "Hikida." Maybe it was good that the tide sounds softened his voice. "Come eat with us, then we find your mommy and daddy." His stomach had started to growl.

Yaeko kept her fingers on her knees. "What they call you?"

Riichiro wasn't sure if the boy trusted them yet. He wondered what the parents had told their son about strangers, about foreigners.

Taking a deep breath, the child stuttered: "Fred-die."

Yaeko had made hinomaru nigiri, round sun rice balls—a red plum preserved in salt and wrapped in white rice. Food like this was never available at the Minidoka camp and Riichiro wondered if that was because the soldiers knew the dish was representative of the Japanese flag. There were also sweet rolled omelet, spinach with sesame seed dressing, and pickled radish and carrot sticks which Riichiro ate hungrily.

Freddie didn't know how to use chopsticks so Yaeko made a kind of plate out of the tin foil so he could use his fingers. When she started to give Freddie half of her share of the food, Riichiro shook his head. He handed Freddie one of his rice balls.

Freddie crinkled his eyes, sniffing carefully. Then he bravely took a bite, slowly rolling the taste around in his mouth and finally swallowing.

"When you hungry, everything taste good," Yaeko told him. "See," she nudged one of the buckets with her foot. "We work hard to dig these up."

Freddie seemed to recognize the shellfish. He pointed at the water with his rice ball. "My dad fishes."

Riichiro spoke in Japanese to his wife. "Maybe he came from the pier. We can start over there." He didn't understand how a father could lose a child.

The three of them watched the tide come in, stretching its thin film and drawing closer up the beach. The dark dots that were people were spread far apart but one was growing bigger into the shape of a man heading towards them.

Yaeko stood up, dusting the crumbs of their lunch off her lap. "Freddie?" she said, pointing.

The boy jumped up and ran towards the man, who swung the child up in his arms.

Riichiro cocked his head at his wife. Together, they walked towards the man and boy.

"I had to go really bad," Freddie was chattering, hand holding tight to his father's. "You said to go over here."

"There was a fish on the line," the man was saying loud enough now to include Riichiro and Yaeko. "What a fighter! When I reeled him in, you were gone!" He scraped away some kernels of rice still stuck to his son's cheek with his thumb and stared at it: "What's this?"

Riichiro stepped in front of Yaeko and stared at the ground. "Hungry boy," he said.

"That's Ki-da," Freddie smiled.

At first Riichiro didn't recognize his name. The boy had cut it short, but he wasn't going to correct him. The father's face and thick neck were burned with sun. Riichiro hadn't brought his broom stick because they'd had so much to carry.

The man stared at Riichiro's boots and work clothes, narrowing his eyes. "Chinese?" he murmured.

So many ways this man was wrong, Riichiro thought, but he wasn't going to say so. He made a small dip of his head. It was just a good thing that father and son were together now.

"They dug clams!" Freddie shouted. "The kind Ma puts on spaghetti."

"Yeah, she does."

Riichiro imagined the father was thinking about his big fish and equipment on the pier. Maybe someone was watching it for him. But now he had his boy and he was losing interest in him and Yaeko.

Overhead, a seagull cawed as the man turned away. "We should go."

Riichiro watched until the two were halfway towards the waterline. That's when he heard Yaeko say quietly, "Goodbye, Freddie."

IV: Yaeko

She didn't like the man's gruff manner with Freddie, the way he pulled on the boy's arm not slowing and waiting for the little one to catch up. She'd seen what Riichiro had not: the stains on his shirt that didn't come from sea water and the hole beneath his armpit. No mother, if she cared, wanted their child to look bimbo—so poor others would look down on him. Appearances mattered.

Riichiro was at the water faucet, rinsing sand off the hand rakes and packing them into a canvas bag he would carry over his shoulder. Yaeko threw the litter of their lunch into the trash and joined him.

She listened as her husband decided to repack their buckets: kelp on the bottom, clams on top with just enough water to cover the shells. Half-full, there would be less chance of slopping over, making a mess on the bus. Yaeko noticed that her pail was packed lighter as if she couldn't carry her own share. But she said nothing. In the restroom, she combed out her hair and redid the rubber band holding the strands in a small ponytail that rested against her neck. With a glove on her right hand to keep the wire bucket handle from biting into her skin, she was ready for the return trip home.

They'd missed the first bus because of the lost boy, and the stop was becoming crowded with people headed home. The sun had broken through the clouds and her cardigan sweater was growing too warm. In the deep pocket was her comb and coin purse. Yaeko waited at the end of the line with Riichiro while the others climbed aboard, the nickels and dimes clinking down the fare box. Last to board, she and Riichiro had to weave their way as they moved from grab rail to grab rail, each carrying their clams in one hand. Some of the riders stared, looking them up and down—from Riichiro's boots and their buckets to the blue-and-white design of her scarf. Some riders didn't move, staring into their newspapers. All the seats were taken as they made their way toward the back of the bus. Passing two men with shiny black hair, Yaeko suspected they were Filipino because of their dark skin. But even they didn't stand to offer their seats to two old people.

Riichiro stopped at the back door, bucket between his boots. He took Yaeko's pail and set it next to his own as the bus slowly accelerated.

Yaeko was glad that someone had opened the windows in the back. The heat of the day brought out the briny smell of kelp and clams. She could see one stocky woman in a suit alternate between holding up an index finger under her nose and waving the same hand in front of her face. Nearby, a man in a short jacket and khaki pants was whispering under his breath. The girl next to him just shook her head. Yaeko glanced out the window to see parked cars flash by. Maybe, she told herself, the man and girl were a father and his daughter. With such unhappy faces, maybe they were having a disagreement about the boy she was dating.

What disturbed Yaeko most were two boys in their early teens in the rearmost seat. She didn't know if they were brothers or friends. But the bigger boy grasped the other's exposed arm with both hands, twisting in opposite directions at the same time. "Indian burn!" he snorted while his victim winced and pulled away.

When the bus hit a bump, Riichiro tried to reach down and steady the two buckets. A small splash had dampened Yaeko's shoe.

"Nah, nah," she whispered to her husband as he pulled out a handkerchief. She bent down to stop him from wiping her feet. He shouldn't be making a fuss. Still, he took time to wipe down the sides of both buckets.

As Yaeko straightened, she felt the elastic waistband of her underwear give way and the cotton suddenly start to slide down, stopping at her hip. She tried to find a pinch hold beneath her cardigan, but her panties skidded further. There was no stance she could take, no way one hand could yank the garment up and keep it in place. Yaeko felt heat rise from her neck like a flare to burn her face. The white fabric pooled around her old shoes. Maybe no one had seen.

Then she heard the smaller of the two boys snicker. The woman in the suit crossed her legs at the ankle and tucked them under her seat, lips forming the word "nasty."

If she fell reaching for the panties, she'd embarrass herself even more. Yaeko lifted her right foot, and then her left to step out of the leg holes. One hand clutching the bus stanchion, she bent her knees the way she had in a long ago obon dance, stooping to bundle her underwear into one hand and slipping it into her pocket. She knew everyone had seen. There was nothing to fully cover her buttocks except the skirt of her housedress. The tires, the bus driver calling out the street names, the hum of the engine—all the noise in the bus dimmed to a throbbing quiet in her ears. Yaeko bit the inside of her mouth to keep from trembling, to keep the wetness welling behind her eyelids from escaping down her face.

That's when she saw Riichiro's hand on the same grab pole as hers. Inch by inch, he slid his fingers down until the bottom three cupped her knuckles while still steadying him on the rising and falling bus floor.

Yaeko could feel her husband's calluses, his dry skin, but his touch was gentle. She took a small breath, holding her chest still: nothing the other bus people could see. Riichiro, she noticed, had turned towards the window, blinking at the scenery, at the Smith Tower—the tallest building in Seattle. Had she ever really seen its pyramid cap, the gleaming white walls and large windows? If she concentrated, Yaeko found she could see clouds of pigeons flying off the top corners.

V: Riichiro

All the way home, Riichiro wanted to say the incident on the bus wasn't Yaeko's fault. It was his for being so poor she had skimped on buying decent underthings. He even had to accept the five and occasional ten dollar bills his sons sent to them from Chicago. But to speak the words out loud meant Yaeko would have to relive that moment. Better not to speak. Better to act as if nothing had happened. Instead, he led her through the alley to the back yard and picket fence around their side of the building.

Yaeko crowded Riichiro as he fumbled with the lock and key, pushing past him through the door when it opened. "Kitanai," she complained, stripping off her cardigan and kicking her shoes into the corner of the kitchen. Then she disappeared around the corner, making her way up to their bathroom. Her tread was heavy, almost stamping as she went up the staircase.

As Riichiro hung up his coat, he heard the faucet turn on, the thrum of water in the pipes. He imagined his wife's skin reddening in the hot bath, her fingers applying a pumice stone to scrub off the sand and sweat and the dead skin of her calluses. Better to leave her alone; he hoped when she was clean she'd feel better.

He wasn't going to dirty Yaeko's floors with his sandy boots. He closed the back door, found two more buckets in the shed and sat himself down next to the outside faucet. The clams needed to be soaked in cold water to filter out their grit. That much he could do. Yaeko had her own way of dealing with the kelp.

Sitting on an old stool, Riichiro reached into a bucket and scrubbed the shells with a small brush, rinsing them, and letting the water filter through his fingers. It was repetitive work and he found himself remembering his grandfather who had been a fisherman. In his old age, the man had played the shakuhachi—concentrating on his breath, the reedy notes hanging in the air. When Riichiro released the clams, each ridged shell plunked into the water.

"Y'know that song?" a husky voice announced.

Riichiro turned to see his neighbor, the mother of the two children next door, on the other side of the fence. She was a generously built woman with full cheeks and rounded arms. In her hands, she carried a foil-wrapped package. He furrowed his forehead. He didn't know what she was talking about or what she wanted.

She hummed a few notes that smoothly went up and down the musical scale.

Riichiro recognized the song from when he'd sat in the back corner of the jazz nightclub. Had he been humming that? The singer's voice that night had stretched out the melody into a refrain. Just at the edge of his memory, the tune troubled him with its dissonant harmonies. Now that his neighbor brought it up, he heard the song again. He started to nod his head with the words she sang.

"...In my pocket not one penny...and my friends, I haven't any..."

Riichiro wiped his wet hands on his pants. He looked down at his boots. Inhaling deeply, he raised his gaze to meet his neighbor's face. He wished he could remember her name. "Black and Tan on Jackson Street," he said. "I hear it there."

For a moment, she looked a little surprised. Then her shoulders shrugged. "Mrs. Hikida around?"

"She washing," Riichiro said quickly. He thought of a naked Yaeko, her washcloth rubbing her neck and shoulder. He didn't want to use the word "bathtub."

The woman laid one hand on the fence. "You know my boys, Hank and Ira?"

Hayes, Riichiro remembered. Her first name was Alverita. Yaeko had mentioned that the first name was a pretty sound in one's mouth.

"Well, I was hoping Mrs. Hikida could watch them for me tomorrow since the school's going to be closed for a whole day because of a water leak." Mrs. Hayes lifted her chin. "This," she said, extending her package, "is for you. Bread I made today."

The foil was warm as Riichiro took it into his hands. He could smell the yeasty dough. He offered it back to his neighbor as he spoke: "Monday, Yaeko go back to work at sewing factory."

There was a low sigh of disappointment and then Mrs. Hayes was raising her hands, "No, no. You keep that. I'll work something out."

Riichiro couldn't think of anything to suggest. "Bread smell good," he tried.

"Yeah, it's just that . . . y'know, I made six loaves because I needed something to punch." Mrs. Hayes pressed her lips together.

He'd seen that look before on Yaeko. It was when she didn't trust herself to control her anger. Riichiro tucked the bread under his arm because he knew he couldn't give it back.

"I got off early from the hospital." Mrs. Hayes explained, both hands resting lightly on the fence post. Her fingers were slim and the nails painted red. "I'm a nurse's aide. Decided to go to the butcher, make a real meal. Oxtails. I took my number, twenty-three, and waited my turn. The counterman, he call twenty-two, then twenty-four, twenty-five." Her voice grew louder as she continued. "So I say, what about twenty-three?"

Riichiro felt a knot in his stomach. He knew this butcher shop. He could see the man's white overalls, the steel-blue eyes, the chalkboard behind the counter, the heavy cash register.

Mrs. Hayes pushed back the hair falling into her face. Then she straightened, becoming taller. "Know what he say?"

He felt himself flinch because now her words were so low, menacing. It was a different way, Riichiro told himself. Not what he would do, but not wrong either. He waited for what he knew would happen.

"He tell me wait my turn and I know he's starting all over again and I'm way at the end of the line if at all," Mrs. Hayes finished. She fanned a hand in front of her face, brushing away a fly. "And then the school called and all."

Riichiro turned to set the foil package on his stool. He fished through the bucket to find the three big horse clams he'd dug up, the oval shells with their blue and brown splotches with the smell of the sea. He wrapped them in a piece of toweling, wondering if Mrs. Hayes knew how hard he had shoveled in the muddy, rocky beach to find them. But maybe she did. She'd given him the bread; he needed to give something in return. "Very fresh," he said, placing the clams into his neighbor's hands. "You make chowder." There was nothing more he could do or say.

He took the bread into his house. From the screen door, he watched his neighbor check her mailbox, walk down the street, and call out "Ira! Hank!" He was sorry neither he nor Yaeko could help out. Maybe there was a relative, a grandmother or sister? Maybe the father could take a day off. But the boys would probably be left home alone on Monday. They'd probably have chores and Alverita would call them from work during her breaks and lunch hour.

Riichiro still didn't know all of the words, but he hummed the strange new song. He felt the notes as they trembled on his own lips, falling and rising and falling.

Blue Jay Feather

Sachi didn't want to hear her husband throw his fist against the wall again.

She'd been late coming home from her senryu poetry meeting; Hatsuji Wada had stopped her, nodding and bowing at the waist, complimenting her water imagery and how subtly a heron slid one raised foot into the tide. Sachi hoped Hatsuji hadn't seen her blush; she'd kept her eyes focused on the tops of her scuffed black shoes. She hadn't felt this way in a long time. Hatsuji had only one small criticism, much too minor to mention as he reached out and placed a thin blue jay feather across her palm. He only offered it because perhaps Sachi hadn't thought about the possible other meanings for the word "feather" or "plume."

Sachi glanced at her purse containing the gift in white Kleenex. The Buick that she didn't like driving was making strange sounds again; the key had to be turned three times before it would catch. Always, she felt like a little girl sitting in the front seat, her right foot confusing the clutch with the brake. On Rainier Avenue, waiting for the traffic light to turn, a car full of teenagers had honked—three long blasts—because she hadn't accelerated fast enough through the green light. Someone was judging her driving at every moment.

Mrs. Langer, the physical therapist, had been waiting. "Not a good day for Goichi, I'm afraid. You know, he's not that bad off. Of course, he doesn't agree. But he's too proud to change." The white woman gathered her things: the funny half bicycle, several different-sized rubber balls, a length of cloth. "I know he's frustrated and tired. But his brain needs to find new ways of doing things in order to start getting better."

Sachi thanked Mrs. Langer over and over. She wished the woman would stay a few minutes longer so she wouldn't have to face her husband. "Tea," she offered. "You work so hard."

Mrs. Langer straightened up from returning the coffee table to its place in front of the sofa. "I know you're doing everything you can, Mrs. Iboshi. But Goichi keeps using his left hand because it's easier. I can't even do massage because he doesn't want me touching him. When I use the pain chart—the ten different stages—Goichi just pushes it away." Her hand on the doorknob, Mrs. Langer shook her head. "It's not right for me to take your money when your husband isn't trying to get any better."

The back of Mrs. Langer's white shirt disappeared into her car. Sachi swallowed; her mouth felt so dry. Maybe Goichi was sleeping. It had been a year since the stroke. She'd made her voice softer, smaller when speaking to her husband. The only time she left the house was for picking up Goichi's medicines, buying groceries, and posting her bills. Twice a week for an hour, she met with eight other men and women to write senryu in the basement of the Ichiban restaurant. The other time was on Sundays when the group had a room at the Buddhist Temple, when she'd told Goichi she was going to church.

The late afternoon sun narrowed into a thinning beam that winked out as Sachi closed the door. She knew she'd be depressed if she had to wake up inside a useless body every morning. Goichi had come to the United States in 1904; he'd worked on the railroads. He cleared land of tree stumps with a mule and dynamite for only ten dollars. His posture had been erect, proud. Now he listed to the right; one side of his mouth drooped. He constantly drooled because he couldn't feel the muscles in his face.

That's when Sachi heard the loud thump, a smack against the wall.

What Sachi wanted most was to pick up the car keys from the pottery bowl in the living room. She wanted to slam the front door and drive away; it didn't matter which direction. But Goichi was her husband. She always came back. Nobody should run away from bad luck. She made herself take a step into their bedroom. "You have a good time with Mrs. Langer?" Sachi asked, picking up a magazine that had fallen to the floor.

Goichi was lying on his side in bed. His right hand was flattened against the wall, all five fingers splayed. He was muttering to himself.

Sachi looked up from his hand to the clock. "Oh, time for your program. I'll turn it on." Her husband loved watching Japanese game shows. That was one of the only times she heard him laugh. Actually, it was more of a series of hiccupping breaths. Their daughter had insisted on the stereo and fine-tuning it to the public broadcast station. "I'll go start dinner. You must be hungry."

As her knife sliced through a seeded cucumber for sunomono, Sachi thought her life was so much different from Hisa's and Shizuko's. It was good to get away from home, to hear other people's voices. The last three meetings, newcomer Hatsuji had sat on her right. Last week, his son had brought him macadamia nuts from Hawaii. Hatsuji gave one small can each to the ladies in their group: Hisa, Shizuko, and lastly to herself. Goichi had sucked the salt from a nut, rolling it from cheek to cheek, finally spitting it out. He couldn't bite down.

Sachi pulled out the cold tofu soaking in a bowl of water from the refrigerator. With some sliced green onions and shoyu, it would be soft enough for her husband to chew. She set the table with cups and dishes, a spoon on a napkin for her husband, chopsticks for herself. Before the war, Goichi's dry goods store was prosperous. They had lived above the store with nice furniture and curtains; they had even sent their two daughters to school in Japan.

She cocked her head, listening to the Japanese words she couldn't quite make out. She could hear the bed creak. That meant Goichi had at least tried to sit up. The huh-huh-huh sound of his laugh was so close to crying. Salting the cucumber, Sachi could feel the sting of a small cut on her index finger. There were things he couldn't do, she reminded herself, but Goichi wasn't dumb.

Sachi tried to keep her mind busy. She'd had such a nice afternoon. Hatsuji had told a story about how he had seen a woman at Maruta's fish store, placing an order for hamachi. Maybe it had been the way she turned her head, the back of her neck curving, rotating like a blue jay. "Mrs. Iboshi!" he had called out. Sachi had bent over, laughing into her right hand, imagining the surprise on Hatsuji's face when he discovered it wasn't her. It had taken Sachi a few moments before she realized that Hisa and Shizuko were only politely nodding their heads. Her friends kept glancing at each other, eyebrows raised.

Poor Hatsuji. He'd told her that his wife had died after a long illness just last March, just before their fortieth anniversary. His square face had looked more tired and drawn without its smile. A year ago, Goichi had been driving the two of them to Shelton to look for matsutake; the smell of the pine mushrooms had filled the Buick.

From the hallway, Sachi could hear the toilet flush. The sound drowned out the voices of the Japanese host and his contestant. Sachi hoped that Goichi hadn't missed the toilet again.

Before she'd left home she had rummaged through her closet, trying on two different dresses, complaining about how much weight she'd lost before pulling on the birthday sweater her daughter had given her and pushing the sleeves up to her elbows. Sachi had touched her wrists and throat with a little

Desert Flower toilet water. As she brushed her hair in front of her vanity, she had seen Goichi's reflection as he watched her. His dead right hand had hovered in the air, the index finger drooping. What did he need?

"Why," he had said, then taken a breath before finishing, "you smile?"

Her wrist rubbed her itchy nose. She could still smell the scent, a little too heavy now because her face was so warm. Why should there be anything wrong with looking well? Nothing was wrong with feeling good about getting together with friends, about not staying home all of the time. Sachi had told him, he should come. Always, he'd answered with a low-throated, insulting "Nyah." It was Goichi's fault they couldn't go out together.

She knew his excuse. Always that weak right side. Back in Japan, there'd been a boy in her class. His left hand had been tied behind his chair to strengthen the right. She'd joined the entire class in his discipline, calling out "Right" whenever he'd raised the wrong arm.

Sachi dipped a finger into her tempura sauce to sample the seasoning. All her life, it seemed like she had only seen the back of her husband's head as he loaded a truck or stacked produce and canned goods. "It's all . . . right," he'd drawn out the word, answering her fears about burglaries in the neighborhood. There'd been the times he paid more attention to a hakujin customer than to the kids, just tousling the tops of their heads before moving on. He had always been a hard worker. Smiling had been for special occasions—New Year's and Christmas, graduations and birthdays and weddings. He didn't smile well; his eyes looked more startled with whites showing all around the irises. Happiness for Goichi was when he landed a steelhead or brought home oysters that she had to shuck. Not that he wasn't a handsome man with a high forehead or that he hadn't given her gifts of flowers or the special Mikimoto pearls on her 60th birthday. Lying in bed with him, she knew he sometimes woke in the early morning before the crows began their ratchet-like calls, and his right arm would thump up and down on the bed because he wanted to hold her hand.

It had been a while, Sachi thought, since she had squeezed back.

Now and then, when Shizuko or Hisa dropped by with fresh baked zucchini bread or extra plums from their trees, they would look at Goichi and shake their heads. Sachi could see what they didn't say with their tight-lipped mouths—*so glad it isn't me.*

The radio had gone on to playing rock-n-roll music. She could hear the tune from a song called "Sukiyaki" that she knew Goichi didn't like. "Papa?" Sachi called, wiping her hands on a dish towel. When she realized that she couldn't hear anything familiar, she hurried down the hall, only stopping outside of the bedroom to peer in.

Her husband was struggling on the floor, the right arm pinned under his chest. He couldn't even crawl. He kept trying to push up, only to fall back down. She put her shoulder under Goichi's armpit, thinking how one of the first actions a baby on its stomach learned was how to flip over.

"What were you looking for?" she asked, helping to prop him up again the wall. Her husband's arms and legs flailed, sticking out in all directions like an untidy bundle of firewood. With a huff, she collapsed beside him. "Nani?" she asked again, glancing at the floor.

What had lain beneath him was her purse. The zipper was wet; Goichi must have used his teeth and left hand to open it. She imagined him wrestling with the strap and fake leather.

There was her wallet, loose change and credit cards, stamps and receipts scattered across the carpet. Sachi felt exposed. Had Goichi read her notes, the scribbled bits of haiku in the white spaces of her grocery lists? Three weeks ago, she had put Hatsuji's address and phone number in the bottom drawer of her jewelry box. Pulling her skirt over her knees, she thought how determined her husband must have been.

Then Sachi saw the feather at the farthest edge of the spill. Sunlight struck the dark shades of blue in the vanes slanting out from the shaft. As Sachi stretched her arm to reach it, Goichi slid into her side.

His face settled onto the ledge of her shoulder. "Me, you— not right," he breathed through the side of his mouth into her sweater.

With tentative strokes, Sachi's fingertips began to brush Goichi's hair out of his eyes. "Remember, the first time I saw Seward Park in the spring? Just married, I was so lonely. Mother, father, sisters—all back in Japan. But the cherry blossoms along Lake Washington! Soft, pink. Petals fell everywhere. You so handsome in white shirt, black suit." Sachi took Goichi's cold hand in hers, and lied: "Blue jays flew there."

Nothing Special

Old guy like me—almost 89—I should snore, sleep deep. Most of the time, I do. But it's hard when the dreams come back. Kind of like the ones about smoking. I quit Pall Malls when a pack went up to twenty-five cents. Cold turkey. Wasn't that hard. Didn't even chew gum or suck hard candies. I did joke around with a box of chalky sugar cigarettes that had Popeye's head in a yellow circle. Then years later, I dream of having a cup of coffee and lighting up. Hold that first inhale deep in my lungs. Then the feeling I shouldn't be doing this, what the heck, and I wake up all guilty.

But these dreams are different, feel more like life. And I know why they started. It's no good to talk about them when you wake up and what once felt so real disappears. All that's left is a feeling of trying to move fast through mud that flows across my tongue, fills my nose and eyes and ears.

Tricia is coming today, I remind myself as I brush the seven teeth left in my mouth that anchor everything in place. I rinse with mouthwash to get the bad taste out and put in the partial plate. In the mirror, my reflection pulls the corners of my mouth into a grin. Pretty good life, I nod, thinking of Maisie and our grown-up two daughters, the seven grandchildren, one great-grandchild on the way. Still remember meeting one son-in-law, Irish-German background. He was nervous and went on about our hydrangeas, the sequoia Maisie's ma started in a coffee can, our koi pond. I didn't crack a smile when I told him we had a nice little Japanese gardener.

I check the bird feeder and change the sugar water for the hummingbirds before going in to breakfast. Maisie puts blueberries and walnuts into our oatmeal bowls. As we eat, we watch for Zinger, Zoom, Zig, and Zag, although I get mixed up between the Anna and the Rufous. Smallest bird in North America. We like their sword-like bills, their aggressive darting through the air.

On the kitchen table, in its black box, is the Congressional Gold Medal of Honor. I haven't opened it since I brought it home three days ago. I couldn't make the big November celebration in Washington, D.C.; the doctors had just put a stent in my arm for renal dialysis. They had to send the medal to Seattle to present it to me while I'm still alive. Senator Murray came to the Nisei Vets Hall to deliver mine. I didn't want a big fuss; I'm nothing special—so there was a nice lunch of Sloppy Joes and corn on the cob. In the background, someone played the piano: "When the Caissons Go Rolling Along." There were red, white, and blue balloons all over the room. At the front row table, me and Maisie sat with the family.

The room went quiet when Senator Murray began: "Despite the injustices of the internment of Japanese-Americans, today's awardee rose above being embittered."

The microphone gave a little shriek and the senator backed away. Several members of the audience winced. Leaning against the back wall was the old boss's son from the jewelry store where I had worked. He must have taken the day off for me. I glanced down at my clasped hands, circling my thumbs.

Murray took a sip of water and continued: "Congress realized in 2010 that soldiers of the 442nd, the 100th Battalion, and the Military Intelligence Service had not been properly thanked and passed a bill awarding regimental members the Congressional Gold Medal of Honor. In battle, Tom Gondo proved that he was a great fighter. In his service, he proved himself to be a great patriot."

Certain words from the speech still stick in my head: "injustices, patriot." Sixty-five years ago, when I volunteered, I was in Minidoka. I had read the recruitment brochure where it said that my service as a Japanese-American soldier would be the best proof against prejudice.

I didn't want praise for my actions. I volunteered because it was something I could do. So much else was shut down around me. I couldn't walk past the barbed wire and guard tower, I couldn't get a job beyond $12 a month as a field hand, I couldn't get more education. I wonder what happened to that young man.

I'm not brave in front of crowds. Nervous about what to say, I kept adjusting my garrison cap to keep it from slipping down my forehead. I had tried to write something that I could read, but I got stuck and ended up with doodles of badly drawn arrows and bullseyes. Everyone stood up as I walked towards Senator Murray and the microphone. I swallowed twice to clear my throat. All I could say was "thank you." Twice so everyone could hear me. I said it to them, the people in the room.

I ask myself now, "Thank you for what?" For recognition and the medal? For the opportunity to serve in the United States Army? For my marching through forests, up those steep, muddy hills in Italy and France? I was a master sergeant and responsible for all my men.

Maisie asks me if I want a warm-up on my coffee. After she pours, I take a big swallow and the liquid burns a path down my throat. When I was in my twenties, I was so angry, and then I was so sad—as we passed for review, those missing holes in our regiment were my friends. My mouth always tasted like blood and iron. My curses confused Maisie, confused my girls. Over the years, I stopped saying "god damn" and "son of a bitch" so much. Instead, I started to point at harvest moons and a young father twirling, wearing his kid's small hooded jacket like a cape. I'd rather see them smile. Most of the time, it was best to be silent.

My family shouldn't have to suffer what I have. They aren't me. Forget about it. A joke will make people smile.

Maisie glances at the clock and reminds me that Tricia will be arriving soon. Our youngest grandchild, an eighth-grader, wants to know more. My daughters knew I had fought overseas, that I had a Purple Heart from when they cleaned out the basement and found the box. My mother had filled it with the letters and photographs I had sent home, even the souvenirs from Europe that I found on leave. There were some copies of the *Stars and Stripes* newspaper about the Mediterranean campaigns, too. Maisie and I haven't talked about those war years in such a long time. But Tricia wanted details, finally calling me and asking for an "interview."

All for an extra credit report about "primary sources"—something about making facts more real. I had wanted to hang up, to say no. I hesitated too long.

Maisie's face looks like it did when I accepted the medal: attentive, but unsmiling. I know she's well-liked, always volunteering for the bazaar and other committees at church. I fell in love with her kindness. She rests her hand on my shoulder and gives it a squeeze.

I'm in the bedroom, digging around in the dresser for a good pair of stockings to wear with my slippers when the doorbell rings. I imagine Tricia giving her grandma a hug; Maisie asking like always, "You being a good girl?"

On the bed, I examine my left foot where the skin is caved in and puckered beneath the ankle bone. I walk just fine, but the old wound looks ugly. Keeping it covered up means I don't have to answer questions about if it hurts. Both feet on the ground, I sit with my fingers spread out at each side and testing the firmness of the mattress.

"Grandpa," Tricia calls in a strident, two-note command.

I wait until the last moment, push off, and head down the hall.

Tricia is emptying her backpack of Hello Kitty notebooks and pens, her ponytail swinging side to side. "Grandpa," she orders and points to the chair opposite her. "You sit there." She hasn't changed much from the bossy little girl who was the teacher when we played school—the type of kid so confident in the belief she knows everything.

Maisie pours tea into two cups and sets a plate of manju with red bean paste centers on the table. Her arm shakes a little. Tricia doesn't know how long it took her grandmother to make this special occasion treat. "Something sweet," Maisie smiles at me before leaving the kitchen.

My granddaughter begins with easy questions like name, place of birth, siblings. I try to tease her like when she was twelve and we used to play poker and she'd called my bluff. One by one, I'd lay out the good cards of my hand like the four parts of a straight: an eight, a nine, a ten, and a jack—building tension. And then the junk card that meant I had nothing. This time, Tricia is patient with me, even though I see her tapping her pencil's eraser against the table.

Today, she's thorough—asking me to repeat what she didn't hear and double-checking her spelling. The small tape recorder goes round and round; I wonder how many cassettes she'll be wasting on me. Then she takes me by surprise as she looks me right in the face and asks: "What did your parents teach you?" At first, it feels like a moment of revenge for all the times I asked what she was learning in school, but she follows this up. "Mom and Dad always say I should be respectful, that I should wait for other people to finish their thoughts before giving mine, to consider their feelings."

After a long moment, I conjure up my okasan and two younger brothers around the dinner table with my father saying that

Saturday we'd spend helping a friend cut up a huge deadfall that came down in a storm. You're Nihonjin, he'd scolded us when we'd groaned, you have to stick together, help each other out. I try to explain this, but something gets lost. She's fourth generation, her father is white, and I wonder what she knows about being Japanese. But she *should* know; we shouldn't have to tell her these things.

Tricia had already done research on the camps and Pearl Harbor. I wonder if she's gone through that box in the basement. She's not asking for a play-by-play history lesson. When I ask her who she's talked to, she speaks in a whisper and glances toward the living room where the television is playing: "Grandma wouldn't say anything except yes or no." Tricia hesitates and adds as if she needs to say something positive: "She did tell me there were good moments..."

I finish for her, "that's where she met me." I break out my big smile that makes my cheeks hurt and for a moment, Tricia relaxes.

"I had to ask Uncle Jiro. He's the one who told me about the loyalty questionnaire."

Of course, I think. My younger brother had friends who had been no-no boys, those Japanese who had resisted the draft, saying no to serving in combat duty and no to renouncing allegiance to the Emperor of Japan. I take a bite of manju before drinking some tea.

Tricia squirms in my silence until she notices the medal. She glances at me for permission to pick it up. I nod, dusting crumbs from my mouth with my fingers. My granddaughter touches the raised lettering that spells out "Go For Broke" and "Nisei Soldiers of World War II." Six soldiers are lined up, rifles resting on their shoulders. In the foreground, another six soldiers in combat gear carry the flag.

I don't like the look of awe on her face. "Pretty, huh? Can't buy that in a store," I say as if joking. My words croak like a bullfrog from the emotions I thought I was holding back. But there it is.

Tricia flushes bright red, dropping the medal back into its case and pushing it to the center of the table. Her hands rest against the edge.

I take a deep breath, reminding myself that she's just a kid. Thirteen? Fourteen? It bothers me that I can't remember. She doesn't know any better. Why? Because no one has told her anything. Isn't that why she's here? We sit in silence for a while.

I start over with a funny story about Camp Shelby, in Hattiesburg, Mississippi, where I had basic training. About how there were two rows of cots lined up and how everyone else had made their beds up with their heads against the wall. "Me," I tell Tricia, "I put my pillow towards the aisle. All the Hawaiians say 'whatsamattayou?' The others—from camps like me—shake their heads, thinking I'm a crazy guy. I explain to my drill sergeant, 'It's because I want the rising sun to wake me.' "

"Oh, Grand-pa," Tricia moans.

I know I've managed to lighten the mood. She sounds like the times when I block her path, my hands held up in the air, and I say "Are you in my way?" I smile and give a quiet huh-huh-huh laugh that's muffled by my closed mouth.

All those games I played with her grandma, her mother, her cousins. I'm a joker, a teaser. I don't say anything about the other diversions I made for myself. The game of "I-know-who-you-were-in-the-war." There was Matt Migita, our television repair guy who lived with his mom and not-quite-all-there brother on a farm in Kent where they'd always plant corn. Matt had been a marksman with an M1 rifle and .45 caliber pistol. Or that Phil Hamanaka, a car mechanic with four kids and a wife who sold Tupperware, had been a battalion runner where the commanding guys would give him a piece of paper that he'd have to memorize word for word. Then, tiny guy Yosh Beppu, best in the league who had bowled two perfect 300 games, 12 strikes in a row. In the war, Yosh had weighed maybe 112 pounds and carried a BAR, the biggest rifle, humping it over the French terrain.

The light in the kitchen is that strong clear sunshine before the sun starts to go down. There's a kind of halo in the room that makes my eyes water. I can't play that game anymore. The years have gone by and we, who survived, have been taken by diabetes or cancer. Or car crashes. The bodies we have are broken, run out of "go."

Tricia flips through the notes. She hesitates, but then speaks quickly. "What was the best advice you got from another soldier?"

I don't know why, but the words are out of my mouth before I can stop them. "Don't stand up," I say. I know I'll have to explain and I don't want to.

My granddaughter cocks her head, just a little tilt.

I take a breath, and exhale. "The Germans," I say, making my voice flat, "had some of the best snipers in the world." When Tricia's forehead wrinkles, I know I have to finish. "When you're a beginner, you tend to poke your head out of the foxhole too much."

I don't go on about how we'd pull a soldier's shirt over his head, pull his helmet down, and stick his rifle in the ground so the graves registration people would see there was a dead G.I. But I do see Tricia's eyes go big when she says, "That means..."

I know what Tricia wants to ask next. Something not part of her teacher's assignment. My face is covered by the Y of my hand, chin resting in the mask of my palm. My breathing is slow: "When I saw death at a distance, I felt sick."

There had been blown-up tanks with their sides scarred from mortar fire. Tree shards. Blood once bubbled from the throat of my battle buddy, pumping out bright red. I could smell the heat of it.

As if from a far-off distance, I hear my voice continue: "But in the moment when death sees you—I had to get them before they got me."

Tricia's hand slides across her paper as she erases the last sentence she's written. She rubs her nose with the same hand.

I figure it's time for me to ask my granddaughter a question: "In the war, we ate C rations. You know what those are?" I use exaggerated hand gestures to show what we had to do as we juggled our gear: "Tiny can of ham that we use a wooden spoon to spread on crackers." I shift in my chair. "Rest time in Italy, we get chicken and rice. Three guys pitch in shoyu they got from home last mail call. Cook everything over a fire. Never tasted anything so good." My granddaughter starts to giggle as I go on. "After we eat, one Hawaiian guy pulls out his ukulele. Then four Italian girls from town come join us. How we dance, even though those ladies are so much bigger than us!"

When we finish, Tricia is quiet. Her mother has come to pick her up. In the doorway, my granddaughter stands taller than me, her shoulder sagging a little from the weight of her backpack. She's probably thinking about what she's read, what she'll double check on her tape recorder. Or maybe she'll just want to hear my voice saying these things. Before Tricia leaves, she turns, her arms surrounding me in a long hug. She doesn't speak. I lean into her embrace that feels like she's holding me up.

After dinnertime and TV, in my pajamas and close to sleep, I go to the kitchen for a glass of water. Maisie left out an old plaid-covered photo album on the counter. Dusty inside and pages are crackly. Here, I see pictures of Camp Shelby—Minoru sitting on the hood of a jeep, his heavy boots resting on the bumper. Us in helmets, holding our rifles with their butts on the ground, the pup tent. And then all of us in uniform, group picture—

Shoji, Nels, Sauce, whole company. They are young and tall and straight. In my mind, they walk to me, pat me on the back linking arms across my shoulder and each other's so that we stand in one big circle. Smiling and cheering, they say, "You old man!" I make big eyes, dropping my jaw like I'm surprised, and say: "What? How that happen?" We all laugh long time.

Kibo's Cats

All the way home from Tuck's Repair, Alice pointed out the new buildings. Seattle was getting bigger. High rise apartments and condos were springing up all along the light rail line. Restaurants like Ichiban were gone. So was the old variety store with cheap fishing supplies, cheap tennis shoes, cheap everything.

Ruriko was gone, too. How long now? Kibo, sitting in the passenger seat, had to count forward from 2005, the year she'd died, to figure it out. It was the same year he'd lost his best friend to a car accident on the floating bridge—he'd gotten a lot of use out of his one good suit that year.

As his sister pulled into his driveway, Kibo felt the jolt in his tail bone—he was glad for his seat belt. Alice wrestled with the steering wheel. "Stupid potholes!"

That was just like Alice to blame the road for her own bad driving. If he mentioned that she had been tailgating or had missed a turn, her lips would mash together in a straight seam and give him a withering look. Never mind that it had been Kibo who taught her parallel parking way back in the fifties. He was the responsible firstborn; she, the spoiled baby sister. It was hard not to think of her as the girl with two pigtails sticking out from the sides of her head. When he looked at Alice now, he saw the same things he saw in his own mirror every morning: crow's feet, age spots, a flabby double chin. They were both old.

At least he could count on her. Family was family, after all. She'd left George at home in front of the television, watching the

PGA Tournament. George was all hot air and he ended his sentences with a fake high laugh. When George was around, everything was about George. If Kibo was sitting in that living room, he'd be listening to his brother-in-law brag about a 25-foot-long putt made eight years ago.

Kibo bit the inside of his lip. It was hard to be nice to George. Alice must have been pretty hard up to marry him.

Alice stomped the brake and the car lurched to a halt.

"Thank you," Kibo said loudly and carefully. Alice was the real reason things got done. But something about his expression of gratitude hadn't sounded right—awkward, somehow forced. He stared straight ahead. His green house with the peeling white trim felt lonely without his car. There was no getting around it: He was going to need his sister's help with transportation for a little while. How could he take a chance with a new-fangled loaner? Who else could he turn to? He and Ruriko hadn't had any kids. Just the cat, Yuki.

He wondered if Alice had heard what he said or if needed to repeat himself. She could hold a grudge for a long time.

"Your lawn needs mowing," she said, her gaze sweeping from the holly tree to the borders of the cyclone fence.

Kibo winced. Her own yard was neatly mowed and trimmed, a Japanese maple shading the porch. But Alice paid someone to do it. She was the type who worried about appearances. He never bothered. The camellia bush was overgrown because Ruriko and Yuki had always looked forward to the spring when robins nested inside.

A black and white cat slid from a warm patch of sun to duck under the side gate, a puff of dust in its wake.

Some cats, Kibo knew, had a sixth sense about people. This one was smart enough to get out of the way. But not the patchy brown cat with the tattered ear on the fence, or the short-haired calico, pregnant again, staring from under the shadow of the stoop.

Clearing his throat, he answered, "Yeah, maybe I'll do some yard work tomorrow." He knew it was the answer she wanted to hear. Instead, he'd be in the kitchen, drinking black coffee and flipping through the newspaper. Ruriko and he used to read the daily advice column out loud.

If he really needed to, Kibo told himself, he could get around by bus, but the stop was a half-mile walk all uphill. He didn't have a bus schedule. And how many quarters was he supposed to drop into the fare box? It had been a long time since he'd caught the bus—back when he was working at the watch repair store, living in an apartment attached to Ruriko's parents' house.

He decided he could put up with Alice if he could keep her outside of the house. He didn't need anyone telling him what to do.

After fumbling with his seat belt, Kibo couldn't find the door lock.

Alice spoke in her no-nonsense tone. "You pay Kenny. I'll send him over."

Kibo had no interest in paying his sister's grandson to mow his lawn, but he nodded anyway. Kenny was the kind of boy, she thought, who needed a job, not a handout. Kibo could remember his own teenage days when he'd work in the strawberry fields with his father, the old man saying not to take a lunch break or else the boss man would think they weren't good workers.

There was no use arguing. Only then did Alice pop the trunk where the two fifty-pound bags of dry cat food lay crowded between her emergency lantern, blankets, and water. Those cats were going to eat him out of his Social Security check. At least he'd found a coupon in the newspaper. For my neighbor, he'd told Alice.

Some things never changed. Kibo slung one bag to his shoulder, thinking that Alice still saw him as her big brother—but the bags were heavier than he expected and he had to lock his hands together, awkwardly kneeing it forward one step at a time.

Alice wasn't laughing. Her eyebrows pinched together. She'd stopped dying her hair jet black, and now it was a cap of white with bangs too short on her forehead.

Kibo stood with one hand leaning against the carport post, the bags of cat food at his feet. "I'll call you when my car is ready." He bent over, stopping to take a breath. When he spoke the words came out one at a time. "You. Can. Go. Now."

Alice held out her hand, palm up. "Give me your house key."

Kibo didn't like the way she was looking at him. Something was wrong. All morning, Alice had nagged at him like he was a little kid. Even though he had set the alarm clock for eight o'clock, he'd still overslept. He was used to taking his time shaving and brushing his teeth after feeding the cats. At least he had set out a golf shirt and a better pair of jeans, not the comfortable old khakis with his beat-up belt that he wore every day. After Ruriko had died, he'd found the bag of old underwear she meant to give to Goodwill and decided nobody could see what he wore under his clothes. The worn-out cotton was good enough for him. It was so soft, so comfortable. But there hadn't been time to wash the dishes still lying in the kitchen sink or wipe off the dining room table. "Nah," he said, straightening up, one hand still on a cat food bag. "No need. George is probably missing you."

Alice opened and closed her extended hand. "C'mon," she said, "I don't like the way you're all out of breath."

Kibo shook his head and walked slowly to his front door. Sometimes, it was just easier to do what he was told. He reached into his jacket pocket, handed over the key, and followed his sister into the foyer. Glancing over his shoulder, he saw two tomcats sniffing the bags of cat food still propped up against the carport post.

Kibo's favorite part of the house was a place in the living room where he could see the birch framed by picture windows. Ruriko used to sit there on the sofa, an afghan tucked around her as she read her crime novels; Yuki, the white cat, nestled on her lap. He sat down hard in the brown recliner and shrugged off his jacket. The upholstery had holes, but it was comfortable; the cushions molded to his body. Alice had gone straight to the kitchen and brought him a tepid glass of water. He sat, counting his breaths until he reached one hundred. Gradually, his heart stopped pounding and he felt a little better as the late afternoon sun flooded the living room.

Water ran from the faucet. His sister was in the kitchen, cleaning up. The refrigerator door opened and closed. Kibo frowned. He didn't want Alice to throw anything out—the milk (which was past its due date but not tasting bad yet), or the hoisin sauce Ruriko had bought so long ago. The sun felt good on his face. If his sister wasn't around, he could lie down and take a nap. Alice was such a gasa gasa girl, like their parents used to say, constantly moving. But it was pleasant to hear someone else in the house.

"You have ants in your sink," Alice yelled at him.

Opening his eyes, he imagined his sister would use a paper towel, trapping an insect against the stained porcelain and squishing the body before rinsing it down the drain. He leaned his head on the back of the recliner and looked out the window into the yard.

In the long grass, little trails led downhill to the three weakened parts of the fence where the cats slipped under to his neighbor's back yard. Kibo checked the crook of the birch to see a half-grown kitten, all black short fur with long white whiskers, watching a bird higher up in the branches. Only the tip of the tail flicked back and forth. It was the same kitten with the rheumy eyes he had tried to clean, the one who wove around his ankles in the early morning when he put the cat food out. Kibo didn't know how long the kitten had to live. It was the last of the litter and looked sick with its big belly, but it had been the biggest, the smartest. He'd buried two others of the litter, victims of the increasingly belligerent raccoons that were taking over. The carcasses had been gutted open, the strings of their intestines hanging out under a cloud of flies. Just last night, he'd seen the hulking mound of a mother raccoon with her four cubs, their sharp eyes reflecting the light over the back door. The drinking water he put out in a large stainless steel bowl had been muddy again.

Alice came out of the kitchen carrying a sandwich on a plate. "Peanut butter and banana," she said. "That banana was starting to go bad."

Kibo cleared away newspapers and old *Reader's Digests* for a spot on the coffee table where she could put the plate down. He didn't think the sandwich would taste very good, but she'd even gone to the trouble of cutting the crusts off. The banana surprised him. He hadn't expected how it would keep the peanut butter from sticking to the roof of his mouth. "Good," he said with his mouth full.

Alice sat down across from him, one hand patting his knee.

Kibo took another bite, chewing thoughtfully. The long held note of a cat's meow broke the silence.

"Come live with us," Alice finally said. "The kids are all grown up. The house is too big without them, but I don't want to move away." She paused, then added, "George has always liked you."

That's what you get, Kibo thought. Being married to George, Alice could only shake her head at her husband as he bragged about the free chicken wings he took home from the all-you-can-eat buffet. Alice must be lonely, he figured—even with her church activities, the grandchildren, her friends. Kibo knew *he* was. He wondered where they'd put him. There was the kid's room in the basement with its own bathroom. It was the farthest away from George. For a moment, he considered that he wouldn't have to worry about cooking or cleaning.

He must have made a face because Alice was getting up. Kibo turned his attention back to his peanut butter and banana sandwich, afraid his sister was going to hug him. He choked on a mouthful.

Gently, Alice patted his back. "Just think about it. Will you do that?"

Kibo reached for his glass, taking a long sip instead of answering. He kept drinking until the water was gone. He could hear four or five other cat voices joining in. Their chirps started off soft but ended louder, more demanding.

Alice drifted away and began pulling off the dead leaves of Ruriko's spider plant that hung in the corner. Sometimes, when Kibo couldn't finish a bottle of water, he'd dump the remainder in. Only because Alice was here did he notice that the plastic pot had split its seam and a new sprout was pushing its way out. She tested the soil between her thumb and middle finger; Kibo knew it would be dry. Then he frowned as she noticed the cats waiting outside. He could feel their eight or twelve faces turned up towards the window.

"Where did you get all these cats?"

Kibo could see his sister's eyes flicking back and forth, growing bigger. "They come, they go," he said, brushing crumbs off his shirt. "Not all the same ones."

It was the way each cat looked up at him, their heads cocked, their meows calling for food. Coming home one night, the reflection of his headlights in a cat's eyes made him stomp the brakes, and the car had slid. Had he hit the animal? Was it bleeding, maybe dying out in the dark, in the thicket of blackberries by the road? He had put out a cardboard box with a beach towel by the back door, just under the eaves of the house and out of the rain. The next morning, the cat was in the box with two kittens.

He should have called the Animal Control people. But he knew what would probably happen to them if he did. Didn't they deserve to live? He should have found them homes but the babies were already too quick for him. And there was that look they all gave him, half begging, half crouching as if afraid they'd be struck, ready to run, but still frozen with hope.

A can of tuna fish, a small bowl of milk. Feeding the cats left-over food he had around the house hadn't been too much trouble at first and he'd told himself the cats would eventually wander away or that he could always stop. From the window, he had watched how many litters of kittens pounce and tumble over each other? Their tiny puffed-up backs and tails always made him smile.

Alice tapped the window with the back of her knuckles. "Hey," she yelled, rapping harder. "Go away!"

"Why did you do that?" He couldn't imagine the cats doing any harm.

"Look there," Alice said, pointing. "At the edge of the patio, under your juniper. Raccoon. A really big one."

Kibo swiveled his chair like a little kid, holding one sticky hand up so it wouldn't dirty the cushion. For a moment, he felt a flicker of fear like he'd been caught. What he saw out the window wasn't anything unusual. The cats were keeping their distance from the raccoon as it clawed the dirt in the garden, searching through old cast-off peanut shells from when Ruriko used to put out seeds and nuts for the birds and squirrels. But it was really the cat food he put out every day that the raccoon was after.

What was he supposed to do? Kibo couldn't sit outside with a shovel to club the raccoons. He didn't like cleaning up after the masked pests or rinsing out the muddy water dish. Somehow, being nice had become too much trouble. The cats and raccoons had worked things out—the raccoons ate first and the cats got leftovers.

Alice sighed. "Our neighbor had raccoons in her chimney! They pulled off roof shingles and left their mess everywhere. Her whole backyard smelled." Alice picked up the folded paper towel she'd brought with the sandwich and nudged Kibo's arm, handing it to him. "This could grow into a bigger problem for you."

Kibo felt a sudden chill down his spine. He pushed himself up out of the chair for a better look, imagining holes dug around the window siding. Pest control people would put traps and poison in his yard. Looking out the window, a young raccoon was grooming its tail next to the fence. Only the black kitten showed any sign of worry, backing away towards the door. The other cats sat dozing around the base of the birch tree or plumped up with their paws tucked under like brooding hens. Kibo didn't see anything to worry about. "That's nothing," he said.

Alice rested both hands on her hips.

He thought of how the raccoons raised themselves onto their hind legs, making themselves bigger. Kibo knew what his sister was thinking. Alice was trying to help. For a moment, he remembered her little girl fingers swabbing a gash on his hand. She was trying to be kind, but her know-it-all attitude annoyed him.

Kibo wasn't worried. How long had he taken care of himself? To make his sister feel better, he'd let Alice invite him over for dinner on special occasions—like birthdays and holidays. In November, maybe they'd go to her church's bazaar. He might even let her clean out Ruriko's old clothes, still hanging in the spare bedroom closet.

"You'd better go," he said. "George will be waiting."

Alice began to pick up the plate and glass, then decided to leave them. She gave a snort of exasperation.

His sister's body was still half-turned towards him. From the shadowed side of her face, he could see light reflecting from her pupils.

He'd caught her in a rare moment when she was between actions, with her hands hanging at her sides. There was pity in his sister's eyes. The sun broke through the shade of the birch tree in bright golden coins. When Kibo closed his eyes, he could still see the sunlight, like red splotches against his lids.

Into Eclipse

Simpson College, 1943
Indianola, Iowa

Ryoko Oyenoki wondered if her study light was the only one on as she stared out at the frosty sheen whitening the branches of the maple trees. Could anyone outside see her scribbling away in her third-floor dorm room? She rested the eraser end of the pencil against her bottom lip as she finished her homework.

This late at night was the only time she thought about her parents. After their usual mess hall dinner of mutton and canned green beans, they'd gather around the pot belly stove and one light bulb. Ma would be trying to knit, unraveling her yarn when she discovered a dropped stitch while Pa tied fishing lures he'd never use but swap with his friends. Bedtime would come early in winter. Ryoko turned the family picture face down so she wouldn't have to see them, her brother, or herself at fifteen.

During the day, Ryoko was busy working in the cafeteria, tutoring, helping out the Social Life Committee, or studying for her classes. Her room was warm, with solid walls. She didn't have to walk three blocks to the bath house for a shower or to use the toilet. There was no wind blowing through her room, and it was actually quiet.

When Ryoko had first arrived after her train trip, she'd felt guilty when she saw Mary Berry Hall, the female dormitory where she was to live. The college president had met her and one other Nisei student, another freshman entering during the fall semester, and escorted them to a welcome reception. Her cheeks had hurt after so much smiling, as she listened to the stories the faculty and board members told about the athletic, music and drama programs.

Her roommate, asleep in her twin bed, sighed, rolled over, and settled deeper into dreams. When Ruth shared her family stories, Ryoko tried not to look stunned. She couldn't imagine having a pastor for a father, someone who had advanced degrees from Yale and who had studied abroad in Palestine. Ruth was helpful, offering up an extra woolen scarf and hat for the winter. Come January, Ruth said, it would be fourteen degrees. Her roommate had even invited Ryoko home for Thanksgiving: "We have lots of room and my mother likes to have a full house."

Ryoko stared out the window at the waning November moon. She didn't want to tell Ruth that winters at Heart Mountain had been even colder. Her family couldn't afford anything more than the free army pea jackets. Her Sears corduroy coat would have to do.

Ryoko rolled her shoulders. She was displeased with her English essay. Crossed out lines striped the pages. Mrs. Westerly wanted the class to write a five-hundred-word essay about a happy time. Except for this chance at college, nothing in the past three years had been joyful. Pa had lost his livelihood as a truck farmer. Her brother's regiment was fighting in Europe. Poor food and mail order clothes weren't good topics. At camp, she'd stayed away from her family, eating her meals with school friends. Young people at Heart Mountain were leaving. Some had gone to help harvest beets and other crops on the farms to help the war effort and make a little money while guys in their teens and twenties had volunteered or waited to be drafted. Thinking about the future was hard. She did some work as a nurse's aide— that's where one of her girlfriends had connections with Student Relocation Council members. Mostly she'd hung out at the social hall, listening to gossip while rereading old magazines. Evenings, she'd attend dances sponsored by the High Jinks Club and come home at night to their barrack after her parents had gone to sleep.

Ryoko knew she was one of the lucky ones who got out. At least, Junko had promised to give her rough draft a look.

Junko's scrunched up eyebrows had shown her reluctance at first. "We're not supposed to congregate," she'd reminded Ryoko with a quick look up and down the hall.

Ryoko didn't understand. "But it will only be the two of us." There were six Japanese-Americans at the college. They met "officially" twice a quarter. Another couple of girls were from the camp in Amache, a boy was from Poston, and another boy was from Manzanar. Junko was the closest to graduation.

"I just want to know if I'm on the right track," she'd murmured under her breath. Ryoko remembered how she'd paused, glancing down at the school's scuffed floor. The application to Simpson College, her letters of reference and transcripts, and especially the background check by the FBI had been daunting. Ryoko wanted so much to make a good impression.

English was her most challenging subject, the one that took up the greatest amount of time. On that first day, Mrs. Westerly had read through the names from the class roster, eyes scanning the room for faces: "Jack Ott, Betty Owens . . ." Then there had been that expected pause. Mrs. Westerly had struggled with her first name, then stared at the roster. Finally her teacher said, "I'm sorry. I can't pronounce this."

Ryoko wanted to hide, to scooch down into her desk and let the broad back of the boy in front overshadow her. Instead, she slowly inched her hand into the air.

"Oh," Mrs. Westerly said, craning her neck to see. "You're a girl!"

Ryoko formed her lips into a small smile, then spoke her name slowly: "I'm Ry-oko, and I'm glad to meet you." She'd had the same problem in the high school she'd attended before the war. It was her parents' fault. Inevitably, every white person she knew would ask: What does "Ryoko" mean?

Even her own mother had no straight answer, making "um" sounds, searching for an explanation. "It depend on how the brush writes the kanji characters." Ma had tried to demonstrate with a stubby pencil, making three vertical lines for "kawa" or river. A box divided into four squares, two on top, two on the bottom was "ta" or a rice field. "For some girls," her mother continued, "it is 'good child,' for other, 'truth.' For you, your father pick 'eclipse' for night you born."

From science books, Ryoko knew of the solar eclipse: the heart of the sun blackened out, and the fiery corona turned into a halo. The one lunar eclipse she'd seen had the Earth's shadow edging out the abalone white of the moon. Then Ryoko could see only the border, not the pockmarked craters she'd studied with binoculars.

Her parents hadn't intended her to go to college; they'd wanted her to find a nice boy, get married, and take care of them like a dutiful daughter. Times were hard, but Ma and Pa were healthy and able. To Ryoko, their Japanese way of accepting camp life seemed like it was holding them back.

She knew she was being disrespectful when, before Ma and Pa had a chance to speak, she'd told them: "You don't have to worry about money. The Student Relocation Council here in camp— they came to me. I have a scholarship and a waitress job. And I'll work summers." Ma had teared up at that, wiping her cheeks with her sleeve, knowing Ryoko wouldn't be back to visit. Her father had waved his hand, as if shooing smoke away from his face. "Go then," he'd said. But there had been something softer about the tone of his voice. Was she wrong, or could her father be proud of her for thinking through such a big decision? She wondered now, how much Pa had been forced to change. Was that why he clung so tightly to the old ways?

Ryoko hadn't told them that Simpson was a little college. What mattered was that a school had accepted her. It was a chance. She stacked her books in a neat pile and turned out the light. Her tired eyes blinked at the light of the full moon.

Ryoko spread out the five pages of her handwritten essay on the table in the library. She felt like all she'd done was put down sentence after sentence. Copying the draft over, she saw that what she had written was like a diary entry—fine for her but not an English assignment.

Junko was already unbuttoning her coat and loosening the muffler from around her neck as she waved at her friends. A chorus of "See you, June" followed the girl into the study. Brusquely, she announced, drawing out a chair: "We have an hour. Let's see what you've got."

Ryoko watched as the other young woman read quickly, her head tilted as her pencil made small tick marks in the margins. The quiet finally made Ryoko ask, "It's really bad, isn't it?"

"What? Oh no, no." Junko took a deep breath and looked up. "When you said your happiest moment was when you left camp, I remember feeling the same way. But then I looked back and saw my parents and younger sisters on the other side of the barbed wire fence, their hands waving that slow back-and-forth good-bye."

How had her own parents reacted? Ma and Pa had walked her to the camp entrance. Her father insisted on carrying her suitcase. He'd taken such careful steps as he crossed the planks laid over the rutted and muddy street. At the gate, each parent had hugged her tight, reluctant to let go. Then she was mounting the bus steps with her train ticket and twenty-five dollars the WRA provided. Ryoko had felt excited. She hadn't been worried about traveling alone. Her hand rubbed the tightness growing in her chest.

Junko moved on to the next page. "It's good that you say you enjoy being challenged by chemistry, that there's Bunsen burners and new equipment here."

Ryoko rubbed her chin. She hadn't been sure. High school at Heart Mountain had been in an overcrowded barrack with every student sharing outdated textbooks. She'd learned typing by putting a cardboard placard on her lap, stretching her pinky fingers to the Q and P keys. The coordination and rhythm came to her only when she'd practiced on a real machine in the Administration Building. But she hadn't mentioned any of that. Ryoko strained to reread the second paragraph left uncovered. Suddenly, she wanted to know. "Where are *you* from? What made *you* happy?"

"This essay is about Ryoko Oyenoki, not me." Junko paused, straightening up in her chair. Quietly, she added: "I'm a California girl." She closed her eyes. "White rice made me happy." She smiled, "Baachan would add ketchup and shoyu and cut-up hot dogs and a raw egg over it all."

Ryoko nodded. "My mom used to make me fan our white rice once she added the vinegar and sugar for makizushi. Before the war, our church would pound mochi for Shogatsu."

Junko kept her eyes closed. "My dad had a new fishing boat. Motor, nets—he took a huge loss during those evacuation days." The wooden chair creaked as she shifted her weight. Her eyes opened as she stared directly at Ryoko. "Probably like your family."

In the beginning, they'd been together. Nothing was like their homey two-story farmhouse. Ryoko, her brother, Ma and Pa—all of them tried to shrink themselves small, to stay out of each other's way. Everyone could hear a burp, a hiccup. Don't fight. Everyone will know our problems. The family only laughed when they'd complained, when living conditions were worse than they could have ever imagined. How happy she'd been to leave.

Junko tapped the page in front of her. "Bad food. Lousy barracks. No hot water in the bath houses. Camp is pretty much the same whether it's Minidoka or Gila River, yes? You need some of those details for contrast, to show why you're happy. People here don't know anything about what's happened to us. Just don't overdo. Remember your audience. Don't make it hard for them."

"But it's okay for the U.S. government to make it hard for us?" Ryoko couldn't believe what she'd said. Someone could be listening. She covered her mouth with her hand like she had in their barrack.

Junko drummed her fingers slowly on the tabletop. "Don't forget why we're here. This is Iowa, away from our families, but we're being accepted into a community again."

Lowering her fingers from her lips, Ryoko asked softly: "What do you do when someone asks, 'Why are you so dark-skinned? I thought you all looked alike.' My chemistry partner didn't know I ate apple pie, chicken drumsticks, and other American foods."

Junko's slower, lower tone emphasized her words, "They don't know." She scooted her chair closer to rest one hand lightly on Ryoko's arm. "That's our new job. To be good models." They sat quietly together. After a few minutes, Junko picked up her pencil again. "Here," she said, "This part is the best, where you thank Simpson College for helping and making you feel at home, that people from Iowa are sincere in their friendships. That will impress your teachers and fellow students. You should elaborate and say how lucky you are to have this chance."

Ryoko hadn't much time between her last morning class on Mondays, Wednesdays, and Fridays for her waitressing duties in the faculty dining hall. Three other days, she started later and worked the dinner shift in the regular student cafeteria. Today, she had to change into her starched white uniform. An hour

before the noon bell chimed, she'd be peeling carrots and potatoes, prepping salads before going out onto the floor.

A small brown package was in her mailbox. Ryoko was surprised to discover a pair of navy blue mittens. An enclosed
envelope held a five-dollar bill. "Your father," her mother's hand-
writing explained in a short paragraph, "had a job." Pa started
the boiler every morning so that the kitchen crew could cook.
He was earning ten dollars a month. The job also meant that her
parents each would get a $3.75 clothing allowance. Every month,
Pa would be sending a little from his paycheck. Ma hoped the
navy blue for the mittens was okay. At first, Ma had thought
yellow would be a bright happy color. But maybe navy blue was
better because it didn't stand out.

Ryoko stuffed the mittens, the letter, and the money into her
purse and ran for the Faculty and Staff Club. Already, Dutch the
cook had pulled a rack of chickens out of the oven and was slicing
parts off with a huge knife. A big pot held the bones, gizzards,
and fat for making broth.

Susie shouted, "Hey kid, we have visitors today from Grinnell
College and Briar Cliff U. You can start spooning fruit cocktail
on those salads."

Lunch began with pouring water into the tall glasses with a
smile and an efficient dip of her pitcher. Ryoko remembered how
in the beginning her arms had trembled because she wasn't used
to so much weight on her big round tray. Susie had been the one
to teach her: Serve from a guest's left using your left hand. Never
reach across a guest. Remove on the right. Susie had sat at a plate
setting and made Ryoko practice until she got it right. When
Ryoko thought about it, even chopsticks had rules.

As Ryoko stood quietly against the wall near the service station, she scanned the crowd. Half of the faculty were older white
men in their suits and ties chattering over their lunches. The
other half were women in dresses with sweaters and jackets.

She was topping off cups of coffee when President Voight waved her over and introduced her to two other important-looking men with receding hairlines and glasses. Men who were the presidents of nearby colleges, she learned. Ryoko gave a little neck bow, holding her coffee pot quietly in front of her.

"This is...." President Voight left his sentence unfinished. But then he recovered with "tell these gentlemen who you are."

Ryoko knew he didn't want to make a mistake mispronouncing her name. He knew who she was, though. President Voight was a kind man who kept a silly New Year's Eve hat students had made him wear hanging on his hat tree in his office. Stanley Konishi, when he'd shaken her hand at their first meeting, had looked her up and down, the sides of his eyes crinkling. At five-feet-one, Ryoko was the tallest Japanese-American girl at Simpson. Even Ma had told her, you pretty girl. In her own way, Ma had warned of men who'd be full of sweet talk. Of people who'd want to be seen with her because she was good looking.

Ryoko's parents would have told her to show courtesy, to bow at the waist or at the very least to dip her head. But that didn't feel right. What would they understand about her college life? Instead, she looked up from under her eyelashes, speaking politely, "It's very nice to meet you. I am Ryoko Oyenoki." After her introduction, she added: "Everyone here at Simpson has been so considerate of me."

President Voight dabbed his lips with his napkin. "She has a study group of girls for chemistry. According to reports from Professor Iverson, all of them are doing very well."

"I like to help," Ryoko started to say. It felt strange to realize that her fellow students thought she had a sunny personality. There had been that moment in the student union building when Fred Hiffenger came into the room saying 'Guys, check out this huge spider I caught!' When he dropped the jar right into her lap, she'd let out an ear-splitting shriek. She'd tried not to be mad while everyone laughed and called her a "good sport." It had been an empty jar with a loose lid.

The man with the spectacles interrupted. "Have you heard about what happened in Idaho? Seems like the local sheriff had to hold some Japanese-Americans in protective custody to keep them safe. Some roughnecks were threatening violence. It's all covered in the student paper, the *Idaho Argonaut*."

She hadn't heard. All she could imagine was an old scene from a Western movie with the six young men and women behind in a cage, standing with their hands gripping iron bars or sitting on a cot.

"I'm sure each of those young people is smart, responsible, and hard working." President Voight paused, then smiled. "As is Ryoko here." He nodded his head. "Ryoko is a wonderful student ambassador of good will."

Everyone at the table seemed to stop forking the squares of their pineapple upside-down cake. She felt herself flush against their stares.

The plumes of their breath floated in the Sunday afternoon after the darkened warmth of the theater. Ryoko blinked, following the others onto the sidewalk. She hadn't been to town since she'd arrived from camp. The five of them had loaded themselves into Harriet's car—a used vehicle her brother had repaired.

The night before, Ryoko had been rolling bandages for the Red Cross with Ruth, Harriet, and two other girls from the dorm while listening to Tommy Dorsey and Frank Sinatra. Two of them cut cotton gauze into 3 ½ x 18-inch lengths while Harriet laid them straight on the table. Ryoko and Phyllis tightly rolled the strips. The four white girls chatted about their classes, the cute boys on campus, and the upcoming holiday.

Ryoko hadn't known what to say when they'd asked how her parents felt about finding a boyfriend and settling down. A lot of girls married after graduation. "Oh, you know," she'd stammered. Ryoko didn't want to say that Ma and Pa had been brought together baishakunin, through a go-between, or that they'd met maybe three times before the wedding. Instead, Ryoko asked how their parents met.

The others even practiced steps to the latest dances like swing when they'd finished. At least Ryoko was familiar with the step, triple step, rock from the High Jinks dances.

"I sure could use a break away from books and studying," Doris said, pulling off her glasses and rubbing her eyes. She had shoulder-length brown hair that softly curled around her ears.

Ryoko thought about the chemistry chapters she needed to review and make note cards of for the test on Wednesday. She needed to do another load of laundry and write a thank-you to her folks, too.

"How about a movie?" Harriet spread open a newspaper. "We can make a Saturday matinee, and you'd still have the afternoon to study." When everyone groaned, Harriet smirked, "Or we can grab burgers at the Lunch Wagon. Maybe drop by Kress Department store?"

Ruth and the other girls had chorused with yesses and "I'm in," while she stood quietly, gathering up the loose threads of the gauze into a pile. Neatly, she stacked the bandages in their box. Phyllis looked at Ryoko. "You're coming, aren't you?"

There hadn't been a way to say no and the five of them had spent the last hour-and-a-half watching *The Phantom of the Opera.*

Ryoko wore her open coat on her shoulders, muffler still hanging around her neck with her mittens in her pockets. She was seated between Ruth and Harriet who had to be shushed by the older couple in the row behind when the lights went down.

A dramatic voice introduced the newsreel: "The Japanese will never crack. They will never surrender. They have got to be beaten until they know they are beaten."

Ryoko felt a chill and drew her coat closer, glancing from side to side to see how her friends were reacting. Doris was putting popcorn into her mouth and chewing slowly. With her skirt and saddle shoes, Ryoko thought she looked more American than a Japanese girl from Japan. Ma and Pa, she and her brother had stood around the oil stove that heated the house, burning her parents' mementos. There'd been the photographs of grandparents she'd never meet, books and phonograph records. Worst of all was her brother's kite, the one shaped like a carp and flown on Boy's Day. The thin rice paper had flamed quickly, receding into ash. She flinched as the U.S. fighter planes shot rounds of artillery. The rat-a-tats made Ryoko jump as the commentator continued: "Bombs fell through the air, guns blazing at the Jap batteries, their chief target." Maybe no one else noticed, but Ryoko saw the signs of four rising suns painted on the cockpit. She just knew it was one for each Japanese plane shot out of the sky. Pulling her muffler over her ears and across her nose, Ryoko couldn't recede any deeper into her seat.

She was thankful when the music harmonies and bright colors of the main feature finally began. Nineteenth century Paris, shiny gowns with low-cut decoupages, and Nelson Eddy's baritone were easier to disappear in. The golden-haired heroine was so pretty. Ryoko knew the Phantom needed to be loved, but between two people tenderness couldn't be forced.

Phyllis and Harriet were leaning intently together, first onto the sidewalk and talking about the big mask reveal scene. "Claude Rains looked crummy, but not, you know, screwed up."

There was something the Phantom had said to the singer that echoed in Ryoko's memory. The Phantom had taken the girl beneath the catacombs of the Opera House and said, "They've poisoned your mind against me. That's why you're afraid." There was something else about the darkness, and it bothered Ryoko how she couldn't recall the whole speech, only parts of it.

"Chris-tine," Ruth was murmuring.

Doris chuckled, her hands stuffed into the pockets of her coat. "Christine, Christine, Christine," she said, her voice growing louder.

Ryoko was glad she had her mother's mittens on, her fingers fisted together in their woolen shell to stay warm. At the far end of their line, she tried the name out for herself. Her mouth puckered and pulled apart with the "Chris" syllable. The "tine," she noticed would show off her teeth.

Ruth was walking backwards in front of her and Doris, so she could carry on the conversation. "I just l-oo-ve that duet Christine and Nelson Eddy were singing together." Ruth joined her hands beneath her chin, opening her mouth and pretending to sing.

Something sharp and heavy struck Ryoko's temple. Her neck cricked to the side, her arms flying out in front of her as she staggered to stop from falling. Ruth was staring at something beyond Ryoko's side view, eyes wide, and Ruth's open mouth didn't look like she was singing anymore. From far away, it seemed as if Ruth was yelling from at the end of a tunnel, "Hey lady, you hurt Ryoko!" Two other shadows appeared at Ruth's side.

Someone, maybe it was Doris, grabbed her arm and helped her sit up on the curb. There was a forest of legs around her and Ryoko could hear tussling—pushing and grabbing. On the ground, below a storefront window was the heavy lump of a rock. Her hand went up to her temple, pressing a spot that hurt, that made a growing wet warm circle soak through to the inside of her new mitten.

"No dirty Jap belongs in this town," yelled a skinny woman in a dark jacket, hair pulled back into a bun, shaking her fist.

Blood drops stung as they trickled into Ryoko's eye.

Ruth seemed tall like the trunk of a tree, with Phyllis and Harriet behind her. "Her brother is in Europe, fighting the Germans!"

Ryoko saw the skinny lady glaring, her forehead pinched between the eyes, her mouth and chin echoing the shape of her frown. Her shoes shuffled a step back. Doris, a nursing student who knew about shock, pressed her fingers on Ryoko's wound, asking if she could see her, hear her.

"Be careful of your clothes" was all Ryoko could say.

Ryoko smoothed the small two-page brochure flat. She hoped her father would appreciate *Fishing Plugs You Can Whittle*. Freddie Hiffenger, the boy who'd pranked her about the spider, had given it to her when she'd asked about trout fishing. Some of the Issei old-timers at camp wanted to try out their home-made fishing poles in the mountain lakes. "You can make Willie Wobble-Tails and Pete Poppers," he'd said. Ryoko didn't think the pamphlet or the carbon copy of Red Cross instructions for knitting socks would be censored.

Outside, tiny specks of snow were starting to fall and twirl from the overcast afternoon sky. Everyone she knew was cramming to finish assignments for Monday. Her typed English essay lay next to her desk lamp.

Once Harriet had driven the five of them back to Mary Berry Hall, Phyllis had fetched towels, alcohol, and a warm basin of water while Doris cut a piece of tape, making a butterfly bandage.

"How old do you think that—that person—was? Anything you noticed that stood out? And what exactly did she say," Ruth asked, gathering facts so she could write a letter to President Voight and their student newspaper. "The nerve of that woman," Ruth exploded, "attacking from behind." She sucked her breath in between her teeth.

Harriet had taken Ryoko's mittens to soak in cold water, to get the blood out. "We'll do the same to both so you won't have one light mitten and one dark colored one," she explained.

"Don't worry, we can curl your bangs to cover up your wound. It'll look good. You have such glossy black hair," Doris said as she gently applied the bandage.

With her friends all around her trying to help, Ryoko felt awkward as the center of attention. "Stick with us," Harriet was saying while the other girls nodded. "We'll make sure people treat you right." The sour note of her attacker's voice was still in her head—like discordant piano keys all struck at once.

Ryoko uncapped her fountain pen. She started writing "Thank you for my mittens. They are already keeping my hands warm." After the period, Ryoko held the pen in the air while thinking yes, yellow would have been a bad color for blood stains. Pen to paper again, she wrote that the five dollars would go to textbooks for the winter term. Her hand stopped.

She wished she could write to her mother honestly about what she felt. But how could she? Ryoko felt like a duck egg snuck into a nest box and hatched by a chicken.

Ryoko remembered how every one of the girls had stopped and gathered on the floor and sofa next to her when she said, "Thank you for sticking up and taking care of me." She paused. "Can I ask everybody something? What do you think of the name, Christine?"

Ruth blinked, "Well, I like it," as she hugged a sofa cushion to her stomach. "Nice that you get to choose." Harriet and Doris nodded.

Ryoko lightly touched her bandaged brow. "What if I changed my first name." She wasn't certain how her friends would respond. Only Ruth used Ryoko's Japanese name and it had taken a lot of practice to get it right. At one point, the more Ruth practiced, the worse her name sounded. Junko had Americanized her name to June because of all the "Junk-o" comments.

"Christine Oyenoki?" Phyllis cocked her head. "Or Chris, for short."

Making her name half American would be easier for her teachers, for life at college. "Christine" seemed to be a part of Ryoko who could help her mix in more easily.

"Hey, Chris," said Harriet.

"Christine, is your head feeling better?" chimed in Doris.

Ryoko giggled.

"Do it!" said Ruth. Then she tossed her cushion at Doris, who batted it away to Phyllis. Soon everyone was blocking or throwing cushions.

The letter to her parents was brief. The windowpanes were icy around the edges. The grass had disappeared. How long would the walkways stay clear? Good things were tricky to write about to people who had it hard. Back in Heart Mountain, everyone would be filling buckets with coal to try to stay warm. At the bottom of the sheet, Christine signed "Love, Ryoko."

The Wind Against Him

Mud had crystallized in the shadows of the tall firs along the fairway. Hank Ide shrugged his shoulders against cold gusts that kept coming out of the northwest, chilling his cheekbones. He dug around in his jacket pocket for a Kleenex to blow his runny nose. Shaking his head, he thought about how he was alone, nobody else coming along. For the thirteenth year in a row, he was going to try his luck at the *Seattle Post-Intelligencer* Turkey Shoot for the $250 competition. Every year, he'd place at least one of his five shots onto the green. Where were the "you can do it, Dad" cheers from his wife and daughters?

Piles of golden leaves hugged the sidewalk edges. He kicked the few near him out of the way, thinking about how he'd worked hard to be a low handicap golfer. Hank had read all the articles by Arnold Palmer and Ben Hogan in *Golf Digest*, studying their form and club recommendations as they competed in the PGA or Masters Tournament. Every weekend, he came down to practice with at least two buckets of balls at the driving range. At one point, Hank had belonged to three different golf leagues until Barb loudly complained that he wasn't spending any time with his family. He'd missed the Blaine Methodist Bazaar where Barb rolled makizushi with the old Issei ladies, and the girls waited tables for the sukiyaki dinner. He'd missed *The Seven Samurai* playing at the Kokusai Theatre, too. But Barb didn't realize that was when he was scoring regularly in the mid-70s like the Golden Bear, Jack Nicklaus. All that practice was good for his game.

"Can't force them to come," Hank mumbled under his breath as he registered for the Turkey Shoot in the clubhouse. The cashier handed him his wire basket and golf balls, nodding Good Luck like she had for all the other contestants. "Salmon!" Hank huffed, as he slammed the door shut and the white explosion of his breath hovered in the air. Who needed an "Arnie's Army"? He'd win this turkey for himself, because he'd been practicing his swing in the basement's family room for months now. The P.A. system barked, making Al Crawford's name a half shriek, half whine.

Waiting in line for his turn up on the platform, Hank stood frowning, his back to the wind, replaying the scene from the morning. He had put on his red V-neck sweater, the one with the Pebble Beach insignia over his left breast, and walked into the kitchen.

Gina was gone. Her bowl, with a few raisin bran flakes still clinging to the sides, was in the sink. At least his youngest daughter had a decent excuse—she and her violin teacher were up in Bellingham for an All State Music Competition. But Beverly had been sitting in her pajamas, idly leafing through a magazine as she spooned yogurt into her mouth. "Is that all you're having for breakfast?" Hank was sorry he'd even bothered to ask when Beverly looked at him, one eyebrow raised as if to say, *You know I'm trying to lose weight for the Homecoming Dance.* That's when Barb had passed him a dinner plate of pancakes, three sausage links tucked in along the sides.

"Mom," Beverly had said, her finger tapping a magazine page folded back to show a skinny model. "This is the dress I want to buy. Isn't that neckline gorgeous?"

Hank had glanced sideways at his daughter, and then at the advertisement. He shifted his attention to his food; girly fashion stuff he didn't understand. Making a pie-shaped cut into his pancakes, he swirled the piece in his syrup before lifting the fork to his lips. Just last night, he and his wife had talked about how Bev should be worrying about college applications, scholarships and SAT scores. The girl was almost a senior and she hadn't even held a part-time job other than the time she'd cashiered at The House of Hong. Even that hadn't lasted more than three weeks.

Hank watched his wife's face as her eyes took in the red-lettered price tag. "Forty dollars!" she sputtered. "You'd better think about babysitting for the Bradleys again, if you want it that badly." Hank was glad his mouth had been full. Beverly's lips had started to seal together in a pouting line, her cheeks glowing pink and round almost like a balloon. It reminded him of Beverly at three years old, her baby-fat face gathering breath for a supersonic scream.

He thought his tone of voice had sounded innocent enough when he swallowed his mouthful, changing the subject and asking: "You ready to see your dad shoot some golf balls?"

With one hand, his daughter had grabbed her magazine, spoon, and empty yogurt cup, standing up to leave the table. "Hardly," Bev had muttered under her breath. In a louder voice, she'd added: "Gotta line up some sticky-handed kids if I want to get anything around here."

"What's her problem," he asked his wife. Barb shrugged her shoulders and they sat in silence, finishing their meal. Barb had only eaten one pancake, alternating between her fork and writing with a felt pen. "We'd better get a move on," he'd finally said, pushing his chair away from the table.

"Oh, Hank," his wife had groaned, gathering her napkin and crumpling it into a tight ball. "I've so much to do. And I've gone every single year. This time, just this once, couldn't you go without me? I really need to finish my menu planning. The house needs to be vacuumed. Company's coming for Thanksgiving. That's this Thursday you know. I do want to make a good impression." She had turned her tablet to show him her plans.

There was a list of names: Minnie and Don Ochi, George Vanderbilt, Miriam Meyer, Leslie Gibson. Most of the people were from the Vanderbilt Accounting Firm where Barb worked as a secretary. Further down, under several crossed out items, the word "salmon" was underlined three times in heavy strokes. He felt his face burn: "But we've always eaten one of my turkeys—one of those twenty-eight pounders."

"They're so big, they always cook unevenly. And they taste dry." Barb had put both hands on the edge of the table, exasperated. "We're having company! It's not just you, me, and the girls. Besides, if you win, we can always put it in the freezer."

Hank clicked his teeth together, imagining the rounded hump of breast, legs, and wings forgotten in the dark of the basement. He blew warm breath on his hands, flexing his fingers, his golf club leaning in the crook of his elbow. There were three players in line before him. A large black man handed the registration sheet to the announcer. His wide back kept bending over after each swing, trying to find better placement for his tee. Each attempt found the ball hooking to the right. The best he could do was thirty-three inches from the hole. But at least the ball had managed to land on the green. The next contestant kept hitting short, and Jinx Yagi who played right before Hank was into the trees.

"No turkey for me this year. Damn, but it's bright," Jinx said as he thumped down the steps of the raised platform, his long fingers shading his eyes. "Clouds cracked open. Wind's even stronger up there."

Hank's first three balls followed Jinx's into the tree line. He felt exposed, ten feet up in the crisp November air. From where he stood, he could see his Chevy parked in the median of Beacon Avenue, the solid square of the Veterans' Administration Hospital and a row of new apartment buildings at the edge of the block. Two women with golf carts passed an old man hobbling

along with a cane. But nobody was watching Hank. The fabric
of his pants flattened out against his legs.

A̲ll the way home, Hank recalled how Jinx had given him a
thumbs-up. How even a stranger like Al Crawford had shaken
his hand while the Turkey Shoot people hustled him towards
the *Post-Intelligencer* banners for a photograph, a quote for the
newspaper and a framed certificate. Hank thought about how
they had given him the golf ball that made the hole-in-one, how
he'd get one of those special glass display cabinets you saw at the
department stores for the living room. Barb and the girls didn't
know what they'd missed.

Glancing at his expression in the rearview mirror, Hank figured he would play it cool. He would ask Barb if she needed help
getting dinner on the table. He'd ask Gina about how she did
at the Music Festival and what piece she had played. He might
even nod his approval of Beverly's two-pound weight loss. He'd
wait until there was a lull in the conversation. No, his day hadn't
been anything special. He'd just made a hole-in-one and won a
two-hundred-and-fifty-dollar gift certificate at Warshall's Sports
Store. Hank imagined the girls screeching, jumping up and down
in their chairs while he smiled and told them to settle down. Barb
would stare at him, her mouth stuck in a little "o" before she'd
stutter, "Wh-Why didn't you say anything?"

He couldn't keep from smiling. After propping up his club
against the trunk of the Chevy, Hank patted the golf ball's round
bulge in his pocket. He tried to pull the corners of his mouth
down with his thumb and forefinger before walking through the
front door.

Barb was in the kitchen. Stacks of cups, saucers, bowls and
plates were scattered across the table. They all had matching
borders of interlacing blue flowers. Barb was busy with a rag,

scrubbing old stains and water spots off silverware. Beverly sat across from her mother, head bowed so that the long black hair hid her face as she fiddled with the magazine.

Later, Hank told himself that he should have seen the signs and backed out of the kitchen. He should have known that some sort of mother-daughter talk was going on. But he'd been almost exploding with his news. He managed to busy himself with filling up a glass from the faucet. Over the sound of running water, Hank caught the angry tone of Beverly's words, but somehow it sounded like all of Beverly's other complaints about how she'd been snubbed by her friends. He noisily slugged down half the glass, then wiped his mouth with the back of his hand. His competition winning hole-in-one, now that was something important. Slowly, he made his way to the table. "What's up?" he asked.

Barb looked up at him and sighed. Hank raised one eyebrow, glancing first at his wife, then at his daughter. "Go on, dear," Barb prodded.

Beverly's fingers busily rolled her magazine into a tight cylinder as she sniffed back her tears. He only caught the muttered words "dance" and the rounded A sounds of a Polynesian name. "What Filipino kid are we talking about? When did you start dating a Filipino boy?" Hank blurted out, shrugging when his wife hit his shoulder with an open hand. "What—?"

Barb spaced her words slowly and evenly. "Beverly's been waiting for this one white boy to ask her to the dance for days now. But he asked a Filipino girl, Debbie Mamallo."

"Oh," Hank said. He sat down with a sigh, sliding the water glass in front of him. The liquid crawled up one side and fell back. "Well, there are *other* boys—nice Japanese ones like Ketch's son. Neil's a nice guy. He's caddied for us lots of times. I bet if we asked, he'd go with you." It was a good solution, Hank thought.

The magazine tube struck the table; Hank jerked back in his chair. Now there was a big dent in the magazine and a bend like a tree branch. "I don't want you to set me up. I don't want to go with Neil. Don't you know anything except *golf*?" The legs screeched against the linoleum as Beverly pushed her chair out. Hank saw Barb's face wince at the sound as their daughter ran from the room.

Hank took a sip of his water. He took a long time swirling the liquid from cheek to cheek. When he swallowed, he looked up at Barb. Then he said: "I hit a hole-in-one at the Turkey Shoot today. I'm going to be in the newspaper tomorrow night."

He hadn't remembered the service being so sloppy at Tai Tung Restaurant. There was a lipstick smear on Gina's water glass. At the table behind theirs, three young men in navy uniforms were telling off-color jokes about ditzy blondes with big breasts. The clientele had obviously changed. Hank and Barbara waited for their food, trying hard to ignore the raucous laughter. When Bev and Gina were little girls, Hank always brought them all for China-meshi after the Turkey Shoot. Shaking his head, Hank smoothed his napkin across his lap; he felt the golf ball in his pocket. Smiling, he brought it out—turning it around and around with his fingers as if it was a globe of the world. "This," he announced to his family, "is it. This is what made my hole-in-one."

Her palm up, Gina reached for Hank's golf ball. Her callused fingers traced the scored red lettering, and she read the word "Titleist" out loud. Carefully she held it up between forefinger and thumb. "Pretty neat, Dad," she said, then tossed the ball back to him. This daughter, he thought to himself. This one who tilted her head, chin aligned to listen to the vibration of the bow string—did she understand about dreams, passion?

He started to say, "You used to carry my wire basket." But Gina shifted in her chair and turned to her mother. Who was coming for Thanksgiving, she wanted to know. His youngest daughter seemed relieved to learn it was only people from Barb's accounting firm. "Maybe Mr. Vanderbilt will promote me to Administrative Assistant. I'd earn a lot more money." Barb stroked her chin thoughtfully and asked, "Do you think I should serve matsutake with green beans?"

Bev sat sullenly, untidy black strands of hair falling into her face. She leaned into one elbow on the table as she played with her chopsticks, writing the same word in water on her empty plate or studying her hand as she opened and closed the two sticks like a chicken's beak.

Gina watched a waiter pass by, then asked: "It had to be that new grip we got you for your birthday. Right, Dad? I bet that's what finally did it." Hank hadn't noticed how tall his youngest had become. She had long thin bones like Barb, and an olive tint to her dark complexion. Smiling broadly to encourage her, he waited for Gina to ask what that hole-in-one moment had been like. He wanted to know, could she still see it in his eyes? "Won't you have something to tell that know-it-all Mr. Fujikake!"

"The wind was against me today, and I wasted those first three balls. At first, I thought my fourth stroke had overshot the green." Hank glanced from Gina to Barb to Bev, who had laid her chopsticks across her plate. He knew he had their attention now. "I wasn't sure I'd judged it right. Felt like maybe too much muscle."

"You mean you got lucky." Beverly's voice sounded low and deep.

Hank snorted through his nose. "Of course not." Then he thought of how the trees had straightened up just for a minute. "Well, maybe a little. But it was practice and skill. I knew what I was doing. It was because I followed through." He turned to face Gina, seated beside her sister. "Like practicing the violin. Isn't it fun when you get it right?"

Gina shook her head: "Not really. I mean it used to be fun when all I had to do was learn the song. Now, Mr. Finkel is always after me about proper chording and holding the bow . . . right." She had let her last word trail away as Hank had begun to frown.

"Girls," Barb began to chuckle. "Remember when your father would hang a string from the ceiling? He'd line himself up behind it and ask you to watch his form—make sure his head wasn't leaning to the side. He tried so hard. Over and over again, he'd ask us if he was straight."

Hank watched as Gina glanced at Bev, who spoke for both of them: "That wasn't any fun for us."

He sat silent as the busboy refilled their water glasses, listening to the ice cubes clinking in the pitcher amidst the laughing voices of the sailors. Under the table, he felt Barb's hand reach for his own and give it a little squeeze. He was glad when the waiter arrived with his big round tray, balancing oval-shaped dishes of pork chow mein, beef with broccoli, special rice, and bean curd with oyster sauce. "Time to dig in." Hank smiled, reaching for a big-handled spoon. "Who wants noodles?"

As Hank was passing a plate to Barb, one sailor's voice grew even louder. Bev's "That's enough" was drowned out as the husky young man waved his hands in the air with a little slip of paper, shouting at his friends to listen as he recited his fortune in a sing-song voice: "'Alas, the onion you are eating is someone else's water lily' . . . and we all know what that means. Right, Big Bob?"

Slowly, Hank set his napkin on the table. He stood up and walked over to the three men. "I'm glad you're having a good time. But could you please settle down and finish your meal." He pointed to where Bev, Gina, and Barb were sitting. "My family's here for our own celebration."

Long after Barb turned out all the lights and he checked the doors, Hank found himself staring at the bedroom ceiling.

Turned on her side away from him, his wife snored softly. She had come into the bathroom just as he started to brush his teeth, his mouth full of toothpaste and foam, to put her arms around his waist. Her cheek had leaned against the spot between his shoulder blades. It had surprised him so much; he lifted his arms up, not knowing where to spit.

"Those boys just got carried away," she had murmured. Hank hadn't expected to feel his heart beating so hard as he stood in front of them. All he'd seen was the black and white of their Crackerjack uniforms. He'd been even more surprised when they apologized. He had felt Barb's lips move. "You know, I'm really happy for you."

Hank lay on his back, hands folded across a stomach that growled, churning with Chinese food. He tried to close his eyes and go to sleep, letting his mind wander to those early days when he'd lost so many balls in the water trap he threw his clubs in after them, screaming curses. And then he ended up soaking wet, even madder, because he had to fish them out. Nothing felt like what he had expected. Hank sighed. With that fourth swing, the club had struck the ball with a meaty sound. Pushing his pajama sleeve up, he rubbed his right arm, imagining the tingle of a good workout. There on the platform, he had squinted and shaded his eyes as he searched the horizon, counting off the seconds it took the ball to fall to earth. Finally catching sight of a black blur, he had watched it bounce high, and with smaller descending hops head for the white triangular flag. Far-away voices, that might have been crows, had hooted. "Ide," the P.A. voice boomed out. "Hole-in-one."

He hadn't believed it. The officials had to tell him a second time. The thought nagged at him like the slow ticking of the alarm clock. The exact curve of his fingers around the grip, the twist and force of his arms bringing the club down—he wanted to remember those things. But all he could recall was the late autumn sun shining red against his eyelids, and the wind blowing through his hair.

Things would have been different, if Barb and the girls had been there. Suddenly, the blankets felt scratchy and heavy. And when he did tell them, nobody seemed to be that thrilled. Nobody really understood. Everyone was wrapped up in their own little world. Hank sat up in bed—his eyes slowly adjusting to the dim light.

Feet, hips, head—the dark shadow of his wife was three big lumps. Barbara's breath was deep and regular. Her nose whistled in a high two-note song. A long time ago, snoring that same way, she'd said the word, "spectacular." When Hank asked, she said she never remembered her dreams.

Acknowledgments

To all of my family and friends who have encouraged me over these many years.

To my big brother, Steve, and little sister, Stacie, who shared the adventures our parents took us on to hunt for mushrooms, to dig for clams, and to fish for salmon.

To my girl cousins for when we'd meet, talk, and reminisce about our parents and grandparents: A.C. Arai, Dale Hazapis, and Diane Bogstie.

To my writing group who have helped shape both my fiction and poetry: John Davis, Susan Landgraf, Robert McNamara, Sati Mookherjee, Arlene Naganawa, Ann Spiers, and John Willson.

To Kate Gray for a memorable week of writing in Lincoln, Oregon.

To Barbara Johns who helped me find contact information on Kenjiro Nomura's artwork.

And lastly, to my husband Michael, who has been with me to talk through the purpose of each story and help me craft the words I write.

Thank you all.

SHARON HASHIMOTO's first book of poetry, *The Crane Wife* (co-winner of the 2003 Nicholas Roerich Prize and published by Story Line Press), was reprinted by Red Hen Press in 2021. Her second poetry collection, *More American,* won the 2021 Off the Grid Poetry Prize judged by Marilyn Nelson and the 2022 Washington State Book Award in poetry. Her poems and short stories have recently appeared in *Indiana Review, Louisiana Literature, North American Review, Pedestal, Alaska Quarterly Review,* and other literary publications. She is a recipient of a N.E.A. fellowship in poetry. She lives in Tukwila, Washington, with her husband, poet Michael Spence, and their two cats.